I0761929

As a child, he'd slept with a nightlight on, but his mother had convinced him it was just his ancestors looking through their belongings; nothing to be afraid of.

Jonathan had developed a healthy respect for his ancestors. After smoothing off the edges of the board, he lifted it over his shoulder and took it with him back into the house.

Stepping inside the back door, he bobbled the board.

She stood there in the doorway staring at him.

Her green eyes locked onto his.

He'd never expected to see one this close up.

"Good morning," she said, her mouth curved into a tentative smile.

He slowly let the board slide down through his gloves until it rested on the floor.

Ghosts were not supposed to speak.

Never. Not once had a ghost spoken in any of the tales passed down by his grandmother, his grandfather, his father, or even his mother, who was sometimes taken to flights of fancy with her tales of ancestors in the attic.

ONCE UPON A CHRISTMAS

ALSO BY KATHRYN KALEIGH

THE BECQUERELS

Twist of Fate

When the Stars Align

Once in a Blue Moon

Once Upon a Christmas

A Wish Upon a Star

Written in the Wind

Scripted in the Stars

Destined in the Twilight

Promised in the Mist

Trapped in the Melody

When Lightning Strikes

Storm of Time

Midnight Storm

When the Moon Falls

Stormborn Angel

Time Tempest

The Heart Remembers

A Moment in Time

Moonlight Shadows

Rescued in Time

ONCE UPON A CHRISTMAS

THE BECQUERELS

KATHRYN KALEIGH

ONCE UPON A CHRISTMAS

A WISH UPON A STAR PREVIEW

Written by Kathryn Kaleigh.

Published by KST Publishing, Inc., 2022

Cover by Skyhouse24Media

www.kathrynkaleigh.com

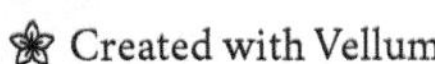

Created with Vellum

To learn more about Kathryn Kaleigh, visit

www.kathrynkaleigh.com

Kathryn Kaleigh

CHAPTER 1

December 1969

Vaughn Dupre woke disoriented. It was nothing unusual. She woke disoriented every day.

She'd fallen asleep after an evening spent listening to Nathaniel read to his five-year-old son, Beau. His three-year-old daughter, Abigail, had already fallen asleep snuggled in her mother's lap. While the parents tucked their two children into bed, Vaughn had gone to her bedroom and crawled beneath the warm blankets.

Now, as she lay here with her eyes closed, she tried to sort out what was different. The sheet pulled over her head smelled… masculine.

Her eyes flew open. Her bed had smelled clean and feminine when she'd fallen asleep last night. Had she somehow ended up in Nathaniel and Martha's bed? She was certain she had not. Yet… the masculine scent was unmistakable. She only knew this because she had spent the last two months as the nanny for Nathaniel and Martha, which sometimes included doing household chores like making beds.

She slowly lowered the sheet and cautiously opened one eye. She gasped.

This was not the room she had fallen asleep in. Gone was the little dresser with the flowers she and Abigail had picked yesterday. Gone was the nightstand with the candles.

Instead, the bed was turned so that she faced the window. The curtains were mere strips of white cloth hanging from the ceiling. Gone were the thick velvet drapes that had been drawn closed when she had fallen asleep.

Suddenly, a loud buzzing filled the air. She threw a hand over her ears and ducked back below the sheets. It sounded like a giant bee.

When the noise stopped, she realized it wasn't an insect in her ear or even in her room.

Quiet as a mouse, she got up and slid off the bed onto the floor. As her toes touched the cool wood, she glanced down. At least her night gown had not changed.

She walked to the window and peeked out.

The buzzing started again.

She gasped and jumped back, her heart nearly jumping out of her chest.

The buzzing stopped and was followed by a loud clatter.

She waited. This time, steeling herself, she went back to the window and peeked out again.

A man, his back to the window, stood below. He was wearing blue trousers and a white shirt. His dark hair was short. He stacked some boards across two wooden platforms, then picked up one long board and turned toward the house.

She moved closer to the tall window, so she could see him better.

As though he sensed her, he looked up and saw her standing there watching him, a scowl on his face.

She froze. Her hands fisted into the cotton of her nightgown.

His scowl changed into a grin. He hoisted the board onto his shoulder, then disappeared inside the house.

Vaughn inhaled quickly and lifted her gaze to the grounds. She was facing the back of the house. The clothesline was gone, as were the clothes she had hung out last night to dry. To her right sat an odd-looking buggy in bright red.

There were no fields of cotton. Just trees where the cotton fields had been yesterday.

She moved closer, grasping the curtain in her right hand.

She jumped back when the grandfather clock began to toll the hour. And faced the room.

Seven o'clock.

Everything was the same, yet different.

It made no sense that she was would be in Nathaniel and Martha's chambers.

She listened closely, but didn't hear the children. Usually by now, they would be up, running down the hallway, getting ready for breakfast.

Then she heard hammering from somewhere inside the house. She needed to get to her room and get dressed so that she could figure out what was going on.

She made her way to the door, then dashed down the hallway, the sound of her footsteps disguised by the hammering. She went into her room and closed the door.

Her heart raced.

The bed was made, but she didn't recognize the green blanket tucked neatly across the top. She'd left her dress draped across the back of a chair next to the bed. Not only was her dress missing, but the chair was gone as well.

She went to the bureau and threw open the doors. Other than a blanket folded neatly and sitting on the top shelf, the bureau was empty.

A wave of panic shot through her, and she ran her hands along her nightgown.

She had nothing to wear.

She turned, and her gaze fell on her reflection in the mirror. She saw a panic-stricken girl dressed in a white shift, her brunette hair cascading around her shoulders. She hurried to the dresser and searched through the drawers, but there was no brush.

She sat on the stool and put her face in her hands.

Then she took a deep breath. After everything she'd been through, she could surely figure this out. She sat up and squared her shoulders. The noise downstairs had grown quiet.

Perhaps that man could help her.

CHAPTER 2

Jonathan tapped the board into place where he had ripped out water-damaged wood and measured for the next. He hammered in another nail for good measure. The old house had been neglected for too long after his father passed away five years ago.

It had taken awhile for Jonathan to make his way back, but now that he had, he wouldn't be going anywhere. It was a little unsettling to be the last of the Becquerel line. He would have to think about what to do with the house when he was gone.

But in the meantime, he had to get her back into shape.

He'd learned to think of the house as a 'she' from his father. His father said the house was a grand lady and should always be treated as such. Built in the early 1700s by Nathaniel Becquerel, it had been handed down from generation to generation.

As far as Jonathan knew, the five years since his father had died was the only time it had been uninhabited. Unfortunately, Henry had been in ill health and hadn't been able to care for her for a number of years even before his death.

Going back outside to cut another board, Jonathan glanced toward his bedroom window.

She was gone.

Seeing her in his bedroom window was a little unexpected, but not a total shock. After spending a year in Vietnam, he was no longer surprised by anything he saw.

Most nights, he woke in a cold sweat, sometimes with his mind blank and sometimes with images of horrors too severe to speak of, but always with his heart racing so fast, it was a wonder it didn't take flight.

As a pilot, he had been shielded from many of the horrors experienced by the infantry. But he had seen his share of carnage. Carnage he had caused, as he flew overhead, releasing the bombs and bullets that downed dozens of men at a time. Sometimes, it hadn't seemed fair. Most days, he was thankful to protect his fellow soldiers, and to keep his country safe by making sure the war stayed on the other side of the world.

That, added to the fact that his grandmother had raised him with tales of ghosts in the Becquerel house, led him to avoid questioning things that could not be explained.

He'd never seen a ghost until he saw her, but he'd heard things. Mostly drums coming from the direction of the slave quarters on a clear still night with the windows open to catch the breeze from the river. Then there was the attic. There were no chains or anything like they showed in the movies, but sometimes, in the dark of night, he would hear boxes, or maybe furniture, sliding across the floor above his room.

As a child, he'd slept with a nightlight on, but his mother had convinced him it was just his ancestors looking through their belongings; nothing to be afraid of.

Jonathan had developed a healthy respect for his ancestors. After smoothing off the edges of the board, he lifted it over his shoulder and took it with him back into the house.

Stepping inside the back door, he bobbled the board.

She stood there in the doorway staring at him.

Her green eyes locked onto his.

He'd never expected to see one this close up.

"Good morning," she said, her mouth curved into a tentative smile.

He slowly let the board slide down through his gloves until it rested on the floor.

Ghosts were not supposed to speak.

Never. Not once had a ghost spoken in any of the tales passed down by his grandmother, his grandfather, his father, or even his mother, who was sometimes taken to flights of fancy with her tales of ancestors in the attic.

And never had a ghost been described as being so lovely that she took a man's breath away. Her dark brunette hair swirled around her face and fell loosely past her shoulders.

"I'm sorry to disturb you," she said, with a French accent. "But I don't have anything to wear."

She swept her hands down her white gown, fisting in the white material. He swallowed thickly as he realized the gown left little to the imagination.

"How are you here?" he asked, forcing his eyes back to her face.

"I awoke in the bedroom," she said.

Not a ghost.

He set the board against the wall and, taking off his gloves, took a step toward her.

She took a step back, alarm on her face.

"Are you a ghost?" He asked.

Her eyes widened. She glanced down, running her hands along her arms.

CHAPTER 3

Vaughn blinked at the man who thought she was a ghost. The thought had not occurred to her. Perhaps she had died during the Indian attack along with Mary and the others in her traveling party.

It was as good an explanation as any. The old Indian had claimed he would save her life by sending her to another time. *You must travel through time. I must send you to a different time.* Vaughn wasn't even sure what that meant. A different time?

But one minute, she'd been in a storm with her traveling companions, dead all around her, and the next she'd been in an isolated field with the sun shining down on her head.

Then Nathaniel had been there and taken her to his home with his wife and two children. Perhaps that had been Heaven.

But if that was Heaven, then what was this? It was the same house, but Nathaniel and his family weren't here. Instead she was here with a strange man who thought she was a ghost.

"I don't know," she said.

He tilted his head and took another step forward. She held her ground.

"You look real," he muttered. "How did you get in the house?"

"As I said, I awoke in the bed," she said, unable to keep the frustration from her tone.

"But you had to come in somehow."

She took a deep breath. He was merely trying to figure this out, as was she. "Yes," she said with a surge of optimism that perhaps he could help her after all. "Nathaniel brought me here."

"Nathaniel?"

"Yes. He lives here, no? And his children, Beau and Abigail?"

The man crossed his arms. "No one lives here other than me."

"But… they were here when I went to bed."

"May I touch you?" He asked.

She felt her eyes widen. What he suggested was improper and scandalous. She took another step back.

"To see if you're real," he explained.

He was back to the idea of her being a ghost then.

"Perhaps you're a ghost," she said.

He stared at her as though she'd suddenly grown horns. Then he laughed.

And she saw how handsome he was behind the week-old beard that covered his face. He had straight white teeth, and she could tell now that he wasn't nearly as old as she had thought.

"Perhaps I am," he said. "And in some ways, I certainly feel like it."

"I'm sorry," she said, unsure how to respond to this man.

"Maybe if I take your hand, we can both see if the other is real."

Empiricism. It fit with Vaughn's practical way of thinking. Empirical and adventurous. That was how she got here, in America, in the first place.

She'd made the decision to go to Fort Rosalie to marry an American. An American she had never met. She knew nothing more than his name: Henry Dickenson. There was nothing there for her in France. She had no dowry and nothing to offer a man looking for a suitable wife. But here it was different. Here, men didn't expect a wife to come with a pedigree. At least that's what the nuns had told her. Unfortunately, she had yet to find out.

"Very well," she said. "You may touch my hand." She held out a hand to him and waited.

Now that he had permission, he hesitated. Perhaps he was afraid of ghosts. Having spent the last ten years of her life being raised by nuns, Vaughn was fairly certain that if ghosts did indeed exist, they were not to be feared. She'd never heard of a ghost who harmed anyone.

With that thought in mind, she took a step forward with her hand still held out.

The man stepped back. What was this? "You're afraid of ghosts," she said, a smile playing about her lips.

"I'm not sure," he said. "I've never touched one."

"It doesn't matter," she said. "Because I'm not a ghost." She studied his face a moment. A handsome face behind the whiskers. "Perhaps you're afraid of girls." She dropped her hand back to her side.

His chuckle had no humor. But as she stepped forward again, he held his ground.

She stopped within arm's reach and extended her hand. His eyes locked onto hers, he reached out, and their fingers touched.

This man was flesh and blood.

He leaned forward and grasped her hand, palm to palm, his fingers entwining with hers, pulling her a step closer. She gasped.

No man had ever held her hand. Her father had, but she'd

been a child. Then she'd lived in the orphanage and touch was something that rarely happened. Besides, there were no men.

He smiled. "I think you're real."

"I think you're real, too," she said.

"My name is Jonathan."

"My name is Vaughn."

"Well, Vaughn, if you're not a ghost, you must have gotten here somehow."

He butchered her name terribly with his southern accent, but hearing him say her name, however terrible his accent, sent a little tingle through her.

"As I said, Nathaniel brought me here," she said.

"So someone dropped you off. Can you call him and have him pick you up?"

"Call him? I'm fairly certain he isn't here." Perhaps Nathaniel was in the field. But even so, Martha should have been in the house.

"But he could come get you."

She stared at him in confusion. Why would she call out for someone who obviously isn't here?

"Do you have somewhere you can go?" He asked.

A surge of panic shot through her. Since her traveling party had been killed, this house was the only place she had known. She had no idea where she was. She had been on her way to Fort Rosalie, but without a guide, she wouldn't know where that was. It then occurred to her that this man could take her there.

"I need to get to Fort Rosalie," she said. "Can you take me there?"

CHAPTER 4

Jonathan released the girl's hand. He was certain now that she was not a ghost, but a real live girl. Here in his home.

What was he supposed to do with her?

Someone had dropped her off. Someone name Nathaniel. And it seemed she didn't know how to contact him.

She wanted him to take her to Fort Rosalie.

Fort Rosalie was a National Park in Natchez, Mississippi, not far from here. Nonetheless, what would she do there? "Why do you want to go to Fort Rosalie?" He asked.

Her chin came up. "I'm to be married."

It all began to make sense now. Fort Rosalie was known as a popular wedding venue. She must have been going to marry this Nathaniel she spoke of.

"To Nathaniel," he said.

She shook her head.

Jonathan was suddenly tired. This woman, who was engaged to someone else, should not be in his house. No matter how beautiful she was, there was no point in her being here. She needed to be on her way.

He turned and picked up the phone from the kitchen cabinet, and dragging the phone cord with it, held it out to her. "Call Nathaniel to come and pick you up."

She stared at the phone, but made no move to take it from him. In fact, she turned away and faced the window.

He groaned and set down the phone.

"I'm sorry," he said. "You don't want to call him?"

"I don't know where he is," she whispered, her head down.

His compassion for this girl returned. This Nathaniel person had probably dropped her off like a stray cat, and now she had nowhere to go. She seemed to be a bit simple-minded. Either that or she was in shock about what had happened to her.

Either way, he couldn't just dump her out of his home. It was a big house, and there was plenty of room until they could figure out what to do with her.

Besides, the weather was about to turn cold, and this rain they had been having could turn icy.

"All right," he said, rubbing his hands on his face. "You'll have to stay here."

She turned and smiled at him. His heart made a little skip. She may not be a ghost, but she was as beautiful as an angel.

She wasn't the kind of girl a man would let go once he had her.

This Nathaniel must be a piece of work.

"I don't have anything to wear," she said again.

He didn't see anything wrong with the dress she was wearing, but he was a little biased. Girls today liked to wear pants about as much as anything else.

"I'm not sure I have anything you can wear, but I'll go look."

"Thank you," she said, relief in her voice.

"You can just… make yourself at home." He swept his hand toward the kitchen. "I'm in the middle of making some repairs, so watch out for nails and such."

Leaving her there in the midst of his construction zone, he dashed upstairs, his mind racing. He and his father had gotten rid of all his mother's clothes after she passed away, then Jonathan had hauled off about ten garbage bags of his father's clothes just last week. He was fairly certain there was nothing left other than his few clothes.

He opened his bureau and rummaged through the clothes he had tossed inside. This really shouldn't be so difficult. He'd had girls wear his clothes before after a night together. Jonathan was no saint and didn't pretend to be, but he'd never been married and, not having any sisters, hadn't paid any attention to the details of women's clothing.

He pulled out some shorts, held them up. They would be too big, but they could pin them up. He pulled out a couple of T-shirts and a button-down oxford shirt. It was cold, so she was going to need a sweatshirt and some sweatpants. There was no way she could wear his sweatpants. They would fall off at the first step she took.

His arms were full of clothing items he hoped she could wear; he dropped them on the bed and started downstairs to get her.

He smiled, then chastised himself for the thought that had just run through his head.

He felt the same excitement he'd felt when he'd gotten a new puppy.

CHAPTER 5

Vaughn closed the door to what she had previously known as the master bedroom. Jonathan had left a pile of clothes tossed on the bed. She automatically began to sort them. There were three white shirts, much like he was wearing, a pair of trousers with the legs cut off, and a light blue shirt.

There was no way she was going to be able to keep those trousers up. She went to the bureau and dug around until she found a long piece of silk cloth that she could use as a belt. She slipped on the trousers and tied the red silk cloth through the loops.

She then removed her night gown and pulled one of the white shirts on over her head. Since it fell to her thighs, she folded it up to create a band around her breasts. It was big enough that she could then loop it into a little knot to hold it in place.

There. She had a chemise of sorts. She put the light blue shirt on last, buttoned it, and rolled up the sleeves.

Standing in front of the mirror, she decided she looked somewhat presentable with the exception of her legs being exposed. There was nothing to be done about it, though, so she ran a brush through her hair and went in search of a chamber pot.

She found it in behind a door in the bedroom. It was a chamber pot like nothing she had ever seen. It was attached to the floor. How did one clean it out?

Curious, she pressed the lever on the back of it and jumped back when water swirled and disappeared.

She put a hand over her mouth and giggled. There was a large bath tub, also secured to the floor. She turned one of the handles and water flowed out of the top and went out the bottom.

This must be the home of a wealthy man to have such a chamber pot and bath tub. She'd always heard that America was a wondrous place, but nothing prepared her for such luxury.

Still in awe of her discovery, she went back downstairs in search of Jonathan.

He was on the floor, a hammer in one hand, a nail in the other. He glanced up when she came into the room and slammed the hammer into his thumb. The string of curse words that followed rivaled any she'd heard from the sailors during her trip across the Atlantic.

She laughed.

He leaned back. "I'm glad you find humor in my misery," he said.

"Not your misery," she answered. "But I must look quite a sight for you to hammer your own thumb."

He shook his hand, but returned her smile. "I'm impressed with what you've done with my clothes," he said, amusement on his lips.

"Merci beaucoup," she said.

He squinted his eyes. "Mercy indeed. How did you get my shorts to stay up?"

"Shorts?" She asked.

He gestured toward the trousers. "Let me see," he said. "How are they staying up?"

She backed away. "I can't show you that."

"Why not?"

"It wouldn't be proper."

"But it's proper for you to be wearing my clothes?"

Feeling the heat in her cheeks, she slowly lifted the light blue shirt enough to grab the end of the red silk cloth so he could see.

He rubbed his thumb with his left hand. "I never did like wearing a tie anyway," he said.

"It's a perfect tie to hold up the trousers."

He stood up. "I should run out and get you some sweats before the roads ice over," he said.

Sweats? She glanced out the window. His language was strange. And not just his accent. Some of the words he used were unknown to her, but she'd expected that when she'd agreed to come to America.

"Do you want to come?" he asked.

She quickly shook her head. Was he suggesting she go in public wearing such a display of clothing? Now she was certain he was addled.

"Alright," he said, "Do you need anything else?"

"A proper dress," she said.

"Yeah, well," he put his hammer on the cabinet and drank from a glass. "No guarantees, but I'll see what they have."

She watched him carefully. Wondered who *they* were. Perhaps there was a seamstress in town who sold dresses already made.

"If you're hungry, you can find something in the kitchen or you can hang out in the living room. I don't have a lot here since I just moved in." His eyes locked onto hers, and his voice softened. "I wasn't planning on having company."

She nodded and, taking his words as dismissal, turned and went into the foyer. The house was so similar, yet different. The grandfather clock was there, but there was a slash across its face. She tilted her head and stepped closer, holding her hand up to it. It looked wounded.

Wounded, but still ticking. She ran her hand along the familiar wood. Nathaniel had shown her how to wind it, so she felt intimately acquainted with the clock. But something had happened to it.

Leaving the clock, she went into the parlor. She didn't recognize any of the furnishings. A plush green rug had been spread across the floor and matching curtains hung from the window. She went to the window and stared out toward the back of the house. It was cloudy and cold-looking outside. Even as she stood there looking out, she felt a waft of cold air from around the window. She needed something other than the short trousers, and she needed shoes on her feet.

The front door closed, and she realized Jonathan had left. A roar came from the front of the house. She ran toward the front window and peeked out, but only saw the back of the buggy. Everything in America, it seemed, was noisy.

Her feet on the cold floor, she dashed upstairs and went back to Jonathan's bureau. Rummaging around through the piles of clothes, she found two matching socks, one on one shelf and one on another. She pulled the socks on her feet, then set about the task of folding and straightening the clothes.

His clothes were odd. He had several shirts like he had given her and several pairs of trousers. All but a couple were of thick blue material that felt rough in her hands. He had eight pairs of white legless garments that made no sense to her.

She sorted and stacked everything – the white legless garments, his socks, his various shirts, and his trousers all on one shelf, leaving one shelf empty. The bottom shelf held a variety of neatly-arranged shoes and boots.

She then moved to the top shelf, also neatly arranged. He had three pairs of black trousers and three large jackets. The jackets each had four buttons and several pockets. The jackets were made of wool and were quite heavy. She pulled one off the shelf and held it up to her. It fell to her knees. Shivering, she shrugged into it and snuggled into its warmth. She shoved the sleeves up and pulled down a box down from the shelf. Cradling the box to keep from dropping it, she pulled off the lid. It was full of what looked to be heavy coins on ribbons. She closed the lid and replaced the box.

Donned in her warm socks and jacket, she went back downstairs.

Halfway down the stairs, she heard an incessant ringing coming from the kitchen.

She followed the sound and discovered that it was coming from the black box Jonathan had held out to her when he suggested she ask Nathaniel to come and get her.

Wanting the noise to stop, she reached out and took the top off the box. It stopped ringing.

As she held what looked to be a handle in her hand, trying to determine what caused it to ring, a man's voice, yelling *"Hello"* over and over, came from the handle.

She dropped the box and the handle onto the floor, turned, and ran back through the house, up the stairs, and to the bedroom.

CHAPTER 6

Jonathan walked around Gibson's pushing a cart through the ladies' clothing aisle, contemplating what Vaughn would need for the next few days during the cold weather. December in Mississippi was unpredictable, but there was definitely about to be a cold spell.

So far, he had three pairs of sweatpants in the smallest size for ladies and was in the process of picking out sweatshirts. She would definitely need smalls. He tossed three in the cart, going with basic colors to match the pants – gray, black, and navy.

She'd asked for a dress, so he flipped through a display of dresses and picked two. One was a yellow-and-white paisley with long sleeves and slightly flared skirt. The other was a similar style but was black, covered with medium-sized polka dots.

He then grabbed some socks before he came to the underwear aisle. Did she need underwear?

It only made sense. If she was here with no clothes, she would need underwear. He glanced around, but there was no else nearby. Jonathan had never bought women's underwear before. He tossed a pack of panties into the cart. One glance at the bra section, and he decided she didn't need to wear a bra. He had no idea where to even begin choosing a size or style in that department.

Shoes. He groaned. He should have asked her shoe size. He rummaged around until he found a pair of boots that he thought might fit her and put them into the cart. Having the basics out of the way, he went to the checkout counter and endured the speculative glances of the clerk. Her name was Mrs. Lawrence. That's all he knew about her other than the fact that she had been working there when Jonathan came to the store as a child with his mother.

From her expression, he could see that if the police came by asking about a missing or kidnapped girl, she wouldn't hesitate to point her finger at Jonathan.

On his way out to the truck, the newspaper headline caught his attention. *Troop Numbers Increasing In Vietnam.*

After a quick stop by the grocery store for bread and other basic food items, he hurried home. It was drizzling now, and it was only a matter of time before the temperature dropped, and they were isolated on the plantation.

Jonathan didn't mind living alone. In fact, he preferred it. Since he had no family left, he'd adapted to being alone.

But the thought of spending time with Vaughn had his blood tripping up a notch. She was quiet and a bit odd, but her beauty more than made up for it. Jonathan had spent four years in college, then traveled the world as part of the Air Force stationed in Vietnam, but never had he encountered a woman so beautiful as Vaughn.

He could not have found a more delightful creature if he had gone looking. But he had just been minding his own business when she had shown up in his house.

He drove down the long, wooded driveway and stopped in front of the house. His arms loaded with bags, he slammed the door closed with his foot and went up the front steps and inside.

He dropped everything onto the kitchen table. The telephone was on the floor, the receiver shooting out a busy signal. He picked it up and set it back on the counter, hanging up the receiver.

Vaughn wasn't downstairs, so he threw the groceries into the refrigerator, grabbed the bags of clothing, and took them with him upstairs.

The grandfather clock chimed the eleven o'clock hour as he reached the landing on the stairway. Vaughn had appeared in his house so suddenly, that he now entertained the possibility that he'd imagined her after all. The whole situation was improbable… unless she was out to rob him. But he had very little of value. Certainly no money around the house.

She must have been a ghost.

The thought came back to him and trashed his good mood. He didn't want her to be a ghost or someone out to rob him or someone crazy who'd just accidentally found her way into his house and then wandered away to the next place.

He wanted her for himself.

He went straight to his bedroom and found her huddled on the bed against the headboard, her knees drawn up and her head down.

He dropped the bags and climbed onto the bed next to her.

She gasped and jerked away.

"Whoa," he said, holding his arms up. "You're safe."

She stilled and looked at him, her eyes round with fear.

"What is this?" he asked, running a hand along the sleeve of his uniform.

"I was cold," she said, and he could tell that she'd been crying.

"It's okay."

He wanted to pull her into his arms to comfort her, but he didn't want to frighten her even more. The sight of her small frame in his military jacket created a strange sense of protectiveness in him. "I brought you some things to wear."

Something had happened while he was out. He'd been gone less than three hours. It was a forty-five-minute drive into town, and it had taken him about an hour to do the shopping.

"What happened?" He asked, though he didn't expect her to tell him.

"Something's wrong," she said, latching her big green eyes onto his. His heart did a little flip. Whatever was wrong, he wanted to fix it.

"Are you sick?" He asked. He would drive her to the emergency room if it would take away the pain he saw in her face.

"No," she said, lowering her eyes. "I don't think so."

"Then what? What happened?"

"I knew things would be different in America, but I didn't realize just how different. It's like a whole different world."

"America?" He asked. She had an accent, but he'd just assumed she was from down south around New Orleans.

"Yes. I came over from France on a boat."

"On a boat. All the way from France?" The very idea was unfathomable to Jonathan.

She nodded. "My friend Mary. Everyone. They were all killed."

Jonathan didn't have television, and he rarely turned on the radio. He preferred to stay isolated. Perhaps there was an accident he hadn't heard about. He hoped Mrs. Lawrence from Gibson's didn't send out the police to look for Vaughn, if indeed, she *was* reported missing.

"Come here," he said, holding out his arms.

She hesitated, but came into his arms and leaned her cheek

against his chest. He realized then just how young she was. How young and innocent. His protective instincts were in full force.

CHAPTER 7

Vaughn allowed him to hold her against him, knowing that it went against propriety. Though she'd just met this man, Jonathan, she had a sense that he was a good man. With everything she'd been through these past few months, she trusted her instincts for that.

She wiped the tears from her eyes and comforted herself with words the nuns had told her before she left the orphanage. *Be strong. God will protect you. This will be an adventure of a lifetime. Embrace it. Go forward and make your place in the world.*

She'd turned seventeen on the trip over. Knowing that she had a husband waiting for her had been comforting. They'd been known as the Casket girls. Girls who brought their wedding dresses with them in their valises. Girls who would marry once they'd reached the new world. She'd had nothing to offer a man in France. No dowry or family to help her find a suitable husband.

It had seemed to be the best choice. Unfortunately, her valise had been lost when the Indians had attacked them, so she had no wedding gown and no idea where to find the husband who was supposed to be waiting for her.

The old Indian had said she would travel through time.

Life with Nathaniel had not been so very different from what she was accustomed to. But now, this house, with Jonathan, was foreign to her. Other than the house itself, nothing was familiar. And what had happened to Nathaniel and Martha? And then there was little Beau and Abigail. Vaughn had been charged with tending to them, but she didn't even know where they were. She missed them. She missed their laughter that had filled the house. She missed Nathaniel's booming voice as he'd picked up his son and tossed him skyward, leaving the little boy screaming in joy.

This house was silent, yet at the same time, filled with so many unknown sounds. Like a voice coming from the handle on a box.

In addition to the sounds, the house smelled different. Older. When she walked into the kitchen where Jonathan was putting in new boards, it smelled more like the house she was familiar with. Only yesterday.

It seemed like such a long time ago. But she was safe here.

Her tears stopped suddenly, and a feeling of calmness settled over her. She lifted her head. "I'm sorry," she said as she shifted away.

"No need to apologize," Jonathan said. "You've had a bad time lately."

She nodded.

"Look at what I got you," he said, dragging the bags from the foot of the bed.

He pulled out soft trousers like she'd seen in his bureau and tops to match. He also had gotten her socks and two dresses.

She took one of the dresses and examined it. She'd never seen stitches so tight like this. Not even the nuns could sew stitches so tightly. The yellow-patterned material was pretty, but the dress was more like a nightgown.

And it was short. He must have bought it from a seamstress who had sewn it for someone else. A child perhaps.

"Thank you," she said.

He seemed so proud of the things he had brought her, so she didn't have the heart to tell him it was too short for her. And he hadn't brought a chemise or a corset.

"I'll go downstairs and make us something to eat while you try it on," he said.

After he had left the room and closed the door, she pulled on the soft trousers. They were stretchy around the waist. She toyed with that a bit, but couldn't figure out how it worked. She left the shirt around her breasts because she didn't have anything else to wear beneath the dress.

She then pulled the dress over her head and buttoned the buttons on the front. She marveled at the preciseness of the buttonholes. This was finer-made than anything she had ever owned. The dress fell to just above her knees. It wasn't so bad with the trousers beneath it.

Straightening up, she found another bag he hadn't shown her. It had a pair of lace-up shoes. She put them on her feet and tied them. Not custom-made, but not a bad fit.

There was package of white garments similar to the ones she'd found among his clothing. Not opening it, she added it to the stack of garments she folded and left on the bed.

After returning his jacket back where it belonged, she took a deep breath and left the room.

Be strong. God will protect you. This will be an adventure of a lifetime.

CHAPTER 8

Jonathan went into the kitchen and made two turkey sandwiches.

When Vaughn walked into the room, he bit his lip to keep from laughing. She wore the sweatpants under the dress, and she must have fashioned a makeshift bra because the dress was a little misshapen around her chest area.

Despite her odd manner of dress, which, he reminded himself, he had given her, she was still beautiful.

They sat at the kitchen table where he ate, and she picked at her sandwich, her eyes downcast.

"I need to finish up these boards before the weather gets any colder," he said.

"Do you want some help?" She asked, her gaze meeting his.

"You? No. I won't be long."

The phone rang as he gathered up their plates to wash. As he picked up the receiver and said "hello," Vaughn watched him closely.

"Captain Becquerel?" Jonathan's commanding officer, Major Thomas asked.

"Yes sir."

"We need you to be on standby."

"Standby?" He echoed, looking at Vaughn, who watched him with an odd expression.

"Yeah. I'm just giving you a heads up that orders are in the works to send us back."

"I see. Any idea when?"

"Looks like it'll be right after the first of the year."

Jonathan scrubbed his face and closed his eyes. "Thank you for letting me know."

"Everything good?"

"Yeah. Just trying to get this house repaired."

"Hunker down, man, there's a winter storm coming your way."

"Got it. See you soon."

"Enjoy your Christmas."

"Thank you, sir. You too."

Jonathan put the receiver down and stared out the window. The trees rustled from the cold wind. *Maybe I should get a television. . . or at least a radio.*

Damn. He'd expected to have a year off, or at least six months, before going back to the Hell that was Vietnam. Apparently, things were accelerating over there, and his company was going back.

Vaughn watched him warily. "You were talking to someone," she said.

"Yeah. My commander."

"You're a soldier, then?"

He nodded and gave her a lopsided smile. "Yeah." He would never go into detail about what he did over there with anyone.

"You're leaving, then?"

"After New Year's. So I'll be here for Christmas."

CHAPTER 9

Christmas. Vaughn was supposed to help Beau and Abigail decorate the tree today. Where were they? Every time her mind flitted near the question, she hit a wall, and her thoughts bounced around in a different direction. She couldn't even begin to fathom what might have happened to them and how this man – Jonathan – happened to be here instead.

All her focus was on him and all the crazy things that were going on. Like him talking to his commander through the black box.

"What is that?" She asked, nodding toward the box.

"The telephone?" He asked.

She shrugged. Nodded.

"This is a telephone. You've never seen a telephone?"

"No," she said.

"Seriously?"

When she didn't answer, he continued to explain. "It's connected by wires to allow people to talk to each other from far away."

The nuns had told her that America was more advanced in

some ways. They hadn't prepared her such novelties as this telephone.

"How do you know who will answer?" She asked.

"Each person has their own number. He turned the telephone toward her. When I want to call someone, I dial their number and *their* telephone rings."

"That must be a lot of numbers."

"It is," he agreed. "I have a book with everyone's numbers in it." He picked up a book from the counter and handed it to her.

She opened the book. It held hundreds of name and numbers. He had some written in the back.

"That's just for people who live close by," he said. "In Natchez. The ones I wrote down are long-distance numbers. Like Major Thomas."

She handed the book back to him. "Everyone does this?" She asked.

"Almost everyone."

"It sounds complicated."

"I can't imagine life without it," he said.

And Vaughn couldn't imagine life with it. To be able to talk to anyone through that black box was the strangest thing she had ever heard of.

"I need to finish up this floor," he said, nodding toward the boards, "then we can do something else."

"I can help," she said.

"It's okay," he said. "Do you know how to build a fire?"

"Of course," she said. Finally. Something familiar.

"If you'll build a fire in the fireplace while I do this, that would be helpful."

Vaughn went into the parlor and found wood already stacked next to the fireplace, as well as kindling. She searched for the tinderbox, but couldn't find it. She did find a box filled with short sticks.

She laid the logs in the fireplace and, taking two pieces of kindling, rubbing them together. Nothing happened. Then she took one of the little sticks and rubbed the end of it against one of the logs. And suddenly she had a flame. *Mon Dieu.* Surprised, she nurtured the little flame until she had a roaring fire.

She was grateful to have something to do. The nuns had instilled a strong work ethic in her. When she wasn't studying and learning, she was doing chores. Along with her native French language, she had become fluent in English. She could also speak some Latin and Spanish and could have conversations in Italian. She was well-read and was proficient in math. She could also play the piano.

When Nathaniel and Abigail had learned of her many skills, they had asked her to be a nanny to their children with the plan that she would tutor them as they became old enough. In exchange, she would receive room and board.

What use would she be to Jonathan?

She flushed at the thought that he might need a wife. She had come to America to be a wife after all. She was to marry Mr. Henry Dickenson of Natchez.

As she got the fire going, she heard Jonathan hammering in the background. It was comforting knowing he was there. If not, she would be alone in this big house.

He said he would be leaving soon. He was leaving to fight in a war. He might never come back.

She sat back and sighed. Perhaps by then, she would find Nathaniel or Henry Dickenson. But how?

She could call them on the telephone. Jonathan had said that he could call anyone on it.

Encouraged, she went back to the kitchen and pulled the phone book off the shelf.

Jonathan had gone outside to cut another board with the loud machine. She opened the phone book and quickly discovered that the names were in alphabetical order by last name. She scrolled down until she found the name Henry Dickenson. She stared at the name.

He was here! In this phone book. If she put this number in, he would answer her. But what would she say to him.

Hello. I'm here to marry you.

She laughed out loud. It was a most insane notion.

She turned the pages and found the name Nathaniel Becquerel. She gasped. How could that be? If she called him, would he come and get her?

Hearing Jonathan come back inside, she slammed the book closed and put it back on the counter.

"Do you need something?" He asked, seeing her standing there.

"Can I have a drink of water?" She asked.

"Of course." He pulled a glass out of the cabinet, flipped a lever, and water flowed out into the glass.

Another wonder.

He held out the glass to her, and his fingers brushed against hers. When she lifted her gaze to his, he smiled. Feeling a little wave of lightheadedness sweep over her, she smiled back.

Jonathan was a handsome man, and his eyes held an undeniable kindness to them.

Feeling guilty about looking through his phone book without permission, she took the water and went back into the parlor.

CHAPTER 10

Jonathan threw himself into the repairs. He had a lot to do before he had to go back to Vietnam. He didn't want to leave the repairs half undone. And now there was the matter of Vaughn. What did one do with a girl who showed up like this?

He took a freshly cut plank and saw that Vaughn had started a fire in the fireplace. He smiled in anticipation of spending a quiet evening with her. They could sit on the couch and maybe read or play dominos.

He whistled as he went out to cut the next board.

As the sun began to set, he put up his tools and went inside. After a quick shower, he went downstairs and pulled the box of dominos from the bookshelf.

Vaughn was on the couch reading. When he walked in, she looked up and smiled. This. This, he realized was what he had been missing.

This companionship without having to take a girl out dancing and entertaining.

"Are you hungry?" He asked.

"A little. Would you like me to cook something?"

"No," he said. "I'll do it."

He went into the kitchen and microwaved some soup he had made a couple of days ago. He found a tray in the cabinet and, after putting two bowls of soup on it, carried it in to set on the coffee table.

"That was fast," she said.

He grinned. "It was left-over."

"Ah," she said, her brow furrowed.

He brought over TV trays, and they ate in silence. "Have you ever played dominos?" He asked.

"Dominos?"

"It's a little like cards, but played with tiles."

"I was raised by nuns," she said, with a chuckle.

"Oh," he said. "Are you opposed then? To playing?"

"Not at all."

They settled across from each other on the floor in front of the fireplace, and Jonathan explained the game. "Does that make sense?" He asked.

She grinned up at him. "I understand," she said.

Then she proceeded to win.

"I have to stop going easy on you," he said.

"No need to hold back," she said.

They played another hand. This time Jonathan played his best. And again, she won.

He watched her, the fire glowing behind her. She played without hesitation. He'd been wrong about one thing. Vaughn was not simple-minded.

On the contrary, she was quite quick-witted.

When the grandfather clock chimed ten o'clock. Vaughn stood up and said, "I need to go up to chambers to rest."

"Are you Cinderella?" He asked.

She titled her head. "Cinderella?"

"Never mind," he said. "I'll walk you to your room."

He knew she could find her own way to her bedroom, but he wasn't ready to be apart from her.

He wasn't sure he would ever be ready to be apart from her.

CHAPTER 11

The next morning, Vaughn woke early and got dressed. She'd had lovely dreams of Jonathan. In the mystical dream world, they had been snuggling in front of the fireplace. Her mind swirled, and then he was comforting her in this very bed after their evening in front of the cozy fire.

Lured by the smell of bacon frying on the stove, Vaughn walked into the kitchen feeling oddly energetic. Wearing the little yellow dress over the long warm trousers gave her a freedom of movement that she was unaccustomed to, except, of course, while wearing her night gown.

She stood in the doorway and smiled at him when he turned to greet her.

"Good morning," he said.

"Good morning."

"I hope you slept well."

"Really well," she said. Vaughn had been exhausted after waking up in a strange place yesterday. A house that was the same, yet different.

"Come in," he said, "Breakfast is almost ready."

Barefoot, she walked toward the kitchen table, but paused to look at a calendar hanging on a nail next to the door.

December. She squeezed her eyes shut. Yes, it was December. It was just much colder than it had been two days ago.

She ran a hand along the calendar, the paper shiny and slick beneath her fingers.

Her fingers stilled over the year. *1969.*

She looked over at Jonathan, whistling as he used a fork to scoop bacon from a stove with a flame. She watched as he turned a knob and the flame disappeared.

She was born in 1697. This was 1714.

Perhaps this was an old calendar and someone had kept it because someone had written the date in wrong. It was doubtless supposed to be 1699. She giggled out loud. Of course. That was it. The orphanage had a calendar dated 1699 that they displayed in the school room. No one saw more than one turn of the century, and many people never saw one at all. Many people lived within the confines of one century or another. The girls were taught the significance of a new century. Vaughn found it amusing that someone had flipped the numbers.

"What's funny?" Jonathan asked as he filled her plate with bacon, egg, and toasted bread.

"Your calendar," she said.

He glanced at the calendar. "Right," he said. "They were giving those away at the bank. I need to get one for next year."

She slipped onto one of the two round chairs with no backs and nodded as he placed a plate in front of her.

"1715 is supposed to be a good year," she said.

"Why do you say that?" He asked, sitting on the other round backless chair.

She shrugged. "I'm here. In America. I'm happy to be alive."

He looked at her with a strange expression. "God bless America," he said.

"Yes," she agreed, her eyes on her plate as she bit into a piece of the toasted bread.

He sat, watching her, as she ate, not touching his own food.

"Are you going to eat?" She asked, nodding toward his plate.

He seemed to come out of a trance and began eating. "Looks like I won't be getting much work done today," he said.

"Why not?" She asked, setting her plate aside.

He nodded toward the window. "It's going to snow."

"Snow," she repeated. The last time she remembered snow, she had been with her parents. The memory was bittersweet because it was also the last time she had seen them.

She had been seven years old, and her parents had taken her out on a sled in the snow. It had been December, like now. She remembered the fat snowflakes and how she and her mother had giggled as they tried to catch them on their tongues.

After their sleigh ride, they had returned to their house. Her father had seen the smoke first. Just a flame shooting out of the fireplace. He'd jumped from the sled and rushed to open the door. Flames had shot out through the open door, but he went inside anyway. Her father's sister was inside. His sister hadn't felt well, so she'd taken a nap instead of going with them on the sleigh ride.

Her mother had followed, and when her father didn't come out, she'd gone in after him. Vaughn had stood there, the snowflakes falling all around her, and waited alone and helpless as her home burned to the ground. Both of her parents had perished in the fire, along with her aunt.

Vaughn had been taken to the orphanage by a neighbor who had seen the smoke and picked her up.

"You've seen snow?" Jonathan asked.

"Of course," she said, putting a smile back on her face. The nuns at the orphanage had taught her that the snow had nothing to do with her parents' death. And that she wasn't to blame either. She'd been a child, and she couldn't save them.

Vaughn had always thought that if they hadn't taken her sleigh riding, they would still be alive. They would all have been home and could have somehow prevented the fire.

The nuns disagreed. They said it was God's will, and she had nothing to do with it.

Vaughn still sat on the fence about that, but she no longer voiced that unpopular opinion out loud.

Living in an orphanage had taught her that believing in fate was more important than trying to sort out things that made no sense.

The telephone rang, jarring Vaughn out of her reverie.

From his one-sided conversation with the telephone, two words stood out for her: Tomorrow and Edward.

He put the handle on the box and turned to face her. "Looks like we're entertaining tomorrow night."

Entertaining. *We?* "Who are we entertaining?"

"My friend Edward from the military."

"Oh dear," she said, unable to hide the panic that enveloped her.

"What is it?" He asked.

"I shouldn't be here."

CHAPTER 12

"What do you mean you shouldn't be here?" Jonathan asked. Vaughn's words touched on the very issue at hand since she'd appeared in his window.

"I'm unchaperoned."

"Edward won't care. He's merely driving through on his way home for holiday leave. He has a wife and child that he's much more interested in seeing than us. In fact, he probably won't even stay long."

"Nonetheless, it isn't proper."

"Fine. I'll tell him we're married." Jonathan wasn't sure where those words came from, much less why he said them out loud.

He couldn't tell his best friend and copilot that he was married. The next time they were flying together, he'd be forced to perpetuate a lie.

"Or that we're engaged."

"You mean betrothed?"

"Yes. To be married. I probably shouldn't tell him we're married."

"That doesn't sound like a very good idea," she said.

"Then what do you suggest?"

"Tell him I'm your cousin visiting for the holidays."

A smile spread across his face. "You're much better at this than I am," he said.

She smiled back. "I was raised by nuns."

He burst into a deep, genuine laughter. "You're funny."

"Maybe, but I'm serious.

"All right," he said, "I'll introduce you as my cousin."

"There's something else."

"What is it?"

"I don't have anything to wear."

"You have your two dresses."

"They don't quite fit properly."

He ran his eyes along her thin frame. With the exception of the sweatpants, the dress seemed to fit her quite well.

"Trust me," Jonathan said. "Edward won't care what you're wearing."

Even as Jonathan said the words, he wondered if he was speaking more for himself than Edward.

CHAPTER 13

"Is there any clothing here that I could borrow? Besides yours." Vaughn asked. Jonathan's friend was coming over tomorrow, and she needed something suitable to wear. Though Jonathan assured her that her dress and soft trousers were the latest fashion, though not necessarily worn together, she felt like she was wearing her nightclothes. She couldn't imagine that ladies wore such dresses out in public, especially not with their legs exposed beneath the short skirt. Only children were allowed to dress in such a manner.

"Pretty much everything went to charity," he said. "Except for a few really old things that might be stored in the attic."

Her hope soared. "The attic? Can we look?"

"Sure," he said, "though I doubt there's anything up there worth much."

Vaughn's excitement was undeterred as they went up to the second floor, down the hallway, and through a door that led to the attic. The orphanage attic had held treasure troves of invaluable objects. She'd had to leave most of it behind, of course, but her wedding dress had been one found in a trunk. She regretted that it had been lost.

Mother Sarah had told her that it was well over a hundred years old.

She followed Jonathan up the narrow stairs, practically humming with excitement.

When they got into the attic, she twirled around. So many trunks! She could spend hours here.

Jonathan laughed. "I've never seen anyone so excited about an attic."

"This holds all the things that were important to people who came before us. It's so very exciting."

"Okay," he said. "Tell me what you want to look at, and I'll move it around for you."

"Everything."

He chuckled. "All right. Where do you want to start?"

She walked around the attic, looking at all the trunks and moving around the abandoned furniture. It was a mystery how they got all these things up those narrow stairs.

When she asked him about it, he shrugged and shook his head.

She pointed to the oldest-looking trunk tucked behind a writing desk. Opening it up for her, he stepped back while she knelt in front of it.

She was quickly disappointed, however, because it only held quilts. Nonetheless, she took each one out and examined it. Then she carefully folded them back up and returned them to the trunk.

The next trunk she chose was full of men's clothing, so she quickly lost interest in that one.

The third trunk she had Jonathan pull forward held more treasures than she was prepared for. This one was packed full of Christmas decorations: delicate glass-blown balls and a fragile faded angel. There were also some little wooden toys, including a boat and a wagon.

"We should put these on a Christmas tree," Vaughn said.

"We could," Jonathan said, "but we don't have a tree."

Vaughn made a face and held a hand toward the window.

"Okay," Jonathan said. "I'll take these downstairs, and we'll go out and cut down a tree."

She sat back and smiled at him. "Thank you."

CHAPTER 14

Jonathan picked up the trunk and carried it downstairs.

A Christmas tree.

With little more than a word and a glance, she had him ready to tramp through the woods to cut down a tree.

Jonathan hadn't celebrated Christmas since his mother had died. After that, he'd been away and there hadn't even been any reason to go home for Christmas. He'd started volunteering to stay on base so others could go home to families.

He barely knew this girl, but she had him thinking of making a home and celebrating holidays.

He set down the box and went back to the attic. She'd opened another trunk and had stood there holding what must have been a red ball gown up to her. His mouth fell open as their eyes met. Right there in this moment, this girl looked like she was in her element. Her face was glowing with excitement, and the dress flowed around her.

"Can I wear it?" She asked.

He swallowed thickly and searched for his tongue. "Of

course," he said. In that moment, he would have granted her anything.

She carefully folded the dress and set it back in the trunk. "Can you take this one down, too?" She asked.

He wasn't sure why she needed the whole trunk, but he lugged it down to the guest room before running back up to her.

As he suspected, she was elbow-deep in another trunk. He went to kneel next to her, curious now.

He felt like the ghost of his ancestors that his mother used to tell him about. This was the first time he'd ever known anyone to actually look in any of these trunks. In his experience, the attic was a place to put things people no longer wanted around.

This trunk was different from the others. Older perhaps, and packed with a variety of things. It looked more like a family's keepsakes than things no longer wanted.

She lifted a piece of paper with a faint gasp.

"What is it?" He asked.

She shook her head. "Nothing."

He shifted to look over her shoulder. It was a child's drawing of a little dog with spots.

She put it aside and lifted the next paper, this time sitting back on her heels, her gaze locked on the drawing.

"What?" He asked.

She didn't move. She seemed frozen.

He reached out and gently took the paper from her hands. He studied the paper, then looked back at her stunned face. He looked back at the drawing.

"This is you," he whispered.

She nodded.

How could that be? How could a drawing of this girl, whom he'd never seen before yesterday, be in a trunk in his attic?

"But how?"

"I drew it."

"You drew a picture of yourself?"

"I know it seems peculiar, but Beau asked me to do it," she said, her voice no more than a whisper.

"It's really good," Jonathan said.

"I'm quite accomplished." Her voice broke with the words.

"That would be an understatement," Jonathan said. He would have to think about the implications of this later. "What else is in there?" he asked, handing the drawing back to her.

She shook her head, her eyes locked on the drawing.

He slid the trunk toward him, curious now about what else could be inside.

There were some embroidered handkerchiefs and a small music box.

He took the music box and opened it. A little trill of sad music echoed through the attic.

There was one item inside. It was a little pin – a cameo.

He picked it up and stared at it. "Look," he said, holding it out to Vaughn.

She lifted her gaze and studied the little pin. She was still as a statue. He wasn't sure if she was breathing.

"It looks a little like you," he said for lack of anything else to say.

When she lifted her eyes to his, they were bright with tears on the verge of spilling from her eyes. "I think it is," she whispered.

She held out her hand, trembling now, and he placed the cameo in it.

She ran a fingertip over the image. "How?" She asked, looking back up at him.

"I don't know," he said.

She closed her hand over the cameo. "I'd like to go to my room now," she said.

"Of course," he said, standing up. He held his hand out to her, and, after she put her hand in his, he pulled her to her feet.

He wanted to pull her to him. To comfort her. But she kept her gaze on the floor.

He was afraid that if he weren't careful, she would break. She seemed like the delicate Christmas balls he'd carried downstairs in the trunk. So fragile she would shatter if not properly handled.

CHAPTER 15

Vaughn sat on the edge of her bed and stared at the likeness of her face on the cameo.

It was disconcerting enough that she'd found a drawing done by her own hand of her own face. She'd sat at the family's dining room table and sketched a likeness of Beau. He'd then asked her to draw Abigail.

"Now you," he had said.

"Now me what?"

"Now you have to sketch one of you."

She'd laughed. "I can't sketch myself."

"Of course you can," he'd argued and jumped up. A few minutes later, he returned with a hand mirror. "I'll hold it," he said. "So you can see what you look like."

She'd laughed again. But the little boy had her heart. If he wanted her to sketch a picture of herself, she would do it.

After she finished, Beau had gathered up all three and taken them to Nathaniel in his study.

She'd heard them talking, but she didn't know what they said. She did know that Nathaniel had sent Beau off to bed, and he had kept the sketches. It was the last she had seen of them.

That had been one week ago.

There was only one explanation. One that her brain wasn't ready to accept.

When her traveling party had been set upon by Indians, she'd been sent from 1714 to 1820.

Had she traveled through time again, this time while she had been sleeping?

Perhaps the calendar hanging downstairs was correct. Perhaps it was indeed 1969.

Someone had saved her drawings – sketches she'd done in 1820 and they had been kept here all these years.

It was plausible, she admitted.

What wasn't plausible, however, was why someone had had her likeness crafted into a cameo.

She studied the cameo again. Perhaps it wasn't her. Maybe it just looked like her. Cameos all looked sort of alike anyway with their ivory silhouettes.

Despite her denials, she knew it was her face. In the picture she had sketched, she'd sketched herself holding a single rose. And unlike most cameos, her face was looking forward. It was an eerily accurate facsimile of the sketch she had done only days ago.

She'd only been with the Becquerel family for two months. She doubted she'd made such an impression on them that they had requisitioned a cameo in her likeness.

She sighed. It was a mystery it seemed that she would never solve. For whatever unknown reason, fate had set her down here.

Little Beau and Abigail were in the past.

I must let them go and move forward.

CHAPTER 16

Jonathan opened the door to the truck and, picking Vaughn up by the waist, set her in the passenger side of the truck. She gasped, but settled herself in the seat, studying the dashboard. She was wearing the sweatpants and sweatshirt he'd gotten for her. Besides that, she was wrapped up in his wool coat.

He went around and got in the driver's seat.

A small, knowing smile played about her lips. "You forgot the horses," she said.

He grinned. "We don't need horses."

She frowned. "You're daft."

He started the motor and she gasped, grabbing the seat.

"It's alright," he assured her.

"What magic is this?" She asked.

"There's no magic," he said. "Just an old truck." The truck was one he'd picked up at a buddy's used car lot for a song and a dance. It was an old truck he could leave if… when… he was sent back to Vietnam. Jonathan missed his Ford T-bird.

He'd sold the T-bird when he went into the Air Force, knowing that his life would revolve around airplanes for the next few years. Besides, he'd wanted to get all his affairs taken care of… in case he didn't return from war. Two of his close buddies hadn't made it home.

One of his friends had left behind a wife and child. Jonathan had promised himself he wouldn't leave anyone behind. It had been easy to do with his parents gone. Jonathan had been an only child, so there was no one. He'd been able to focus on his military career. He been given an Air Medal among a few other medals which were hidden away in a shoebox in his bureau.

Without someone to share them with, they meant nothing.

He glanced over at Vaughn, whose eyes were glued to the road in front of them, her gaze intent. Perhaps someday he could show his medals to her.

The thought sent off a trigger of alarm. Jonathan had no family. No ties. His family was the Air Force.

Emotional ties would be distracting. His commander's words from basic training came clearly back to him. *The Air Force is now your wife, your mistress, and your girlfriend. Don't even think about another woman. The Air Force is a jealous woman, and she requires all your attention from here on out.*

Jonathan knew better, just as he'd known better at the time, but the words were etched into his brain.

He'd lived by them for eight long years now.

"What makes it go?" Vaughn asked.

He looked over at her, her eyes bright with fascination as he steered the truck out onto the dirt road.

His commitment to the Air Force forgotten, he smiled. She was a blank slate, and he wanted to show her everything. "It has a motor," he explained. "The simplest explanation is that I control the speed with my feet and steer it with this wheel."

She sat forward, watching with obvious fascination. "Does everyone travel like this?" She asked.

He thought about the airplanes that he flew, buses, and trains, but went with the simplest answer. "Yes," he said.

"No more horses?"

"A few people have them, but they ride them for fun."

No more horses. So the girl had expected to travel by horse. He'd heard of communities that still used horses and buggies. What were they? Mennonites? Or Amish? It all suddenly made sense to him. She wasn't familiar with the telephone or the car, or any other of the obvious trappings of modern life.

There were many possible explanations for how she came to be here. Maybe she'd been kidnapped and dropped off here. Or maybe she'd lost her memory and somehow ended up here.

Whatever it was, he considered it divine intervention that she'd landed in his bedroom and not somewhere that would put her in danger.

Jonathan would protect her until she figured out where she belonged.

The idea of her figuring that out put a scowl on his face.

He wanted her to belong here – with him.

CHAPTER 17

Vaughn peered out the front of what Jonathan called the truck. She had never seen such a wonder as this. This conveyance… this *truck* was almost magical. Like sledding down a snowy hill. Except there was no snow, and there was no hill. They were gliding along a dirt road as though there was nothing to it.

When Jonathan had suggested they go out to look for a Christmas tree, she'd put on the warmest clothes she could find.

His friend was coming to visit tonight, so she was saving the blue dress she'd found in the trunk for that occasion. It was going to be a surprise for Jonathan. She couldn't wait to dress properly as she was accustomed to.

She pushed aside the thought that the long blue ball gown might not be proper dress for 1969, if indeed that's where she was.

Jonathan pulled the truck off the side of the road and turned off the motor.

"There should be a good tree out here," he said, nodding toward a grove of trees. "I'll come around."

While she waited, he came around the truck, opened the door, and helped her out. After he set her firmly on her feet, he kept his hands on her waist. She blinked and lifted her chin until her eyes met his.

The cold air swirled around them, sending a shiver through her. Gazing into his blue eyes, she forgot about the possibility of being in a different time. She forgot to worry about what appropriate fashion was.

She saw only his crooked grin as he stared into her eyes.

Another one of those trucks passed by, this one going much faster. Jonathan lifted a hand and waved as the driver passed.

"Come on," Jonathan said after he grabbed an ax from the back of the truck and tossed it over his shoulder. "Let's go find us a Christmas tree."

Vaughn had spent some time in the woods growing up. The nuns insisted on a daily walk, weather permitting. Their walks, however, were on a smooth pathway. Not through the woods with no path and no direction.

Jonathan stepped over a log and took her hand to help her over.

"Where are we going?" She asked.

"I remember some nice trees over this way."

"Can you find your way back?" She asked. She saw no landmarks to give them direction, and with the cloudy sky, there was no sunlight to follow.

"Of course," he said. "I used to hunt here all the time."

"You no longer hunt?" She asked.

"Rarely."

"Then how do you get food?"

He glanced at her oddly, but said. "I purchase it."

"Ah." Of course. That's what the nuns did. She wasn't sure how her father acquired food for her and her mother before they were killed. She had no memory of him either going hunting or coming home with game. As a child, she'd had no reason to be concerned with where her meals came from.

Suddenly, Jonathan stopped and looked to his left.

Vaughn stopped also and followed his gaze.

She was unprepared for what she saw.

CHAPTER 18

One of Jonathan's earliest memories was of walking through these woods with his father, Bradford Becquerel.

Bradford had an entrepreneurial spirit. For one, he'd planted acres of Fraser fir trees.

Someday, Jonathan, these trees will all be yours. They'll be worth something someday.

Jonathan had put the trees in the back of his mind as he'd attended college, then flight school, and finally had gone to Vietnam.

Now, with Vaughn, he'd remembered that he had a grove of Christmas trees on his very own land. Considering that they had been left unattended for nearly fifteen years, the seedlings had grown up nicely.

"They're lovely," Vaughn said.

"My father planted them," Jonathan said, proudly.

"Which one do we get?"

"You pick," he said. "Pick out any one, and I'll chop it down."

Her eyes bright, she walked among the trees, one hand outstretched to run along the branches as she passed.

He followed, watching her.

He was enchanted. Everything looked different through her eyes. It looked new and shiny.

The trees had gotten too big. He should have cut them years ago and sold them. Unfortunately, running a tree farm had never been one of his life goals.

But with Vaughn… everything looked different.

Maybe when he came back from his tour in Vietnam… His service with the Air Force would be completed. Maybe they could fix up the Christmas tree farm and, with just a little word of mouth, make a go of it.

"I like this one," Vaughn said, both hands on the branches of one of the taller trees, a smile across her face.

"I like this one, too," Jonathan said, but he was looking at Vaughn, not the tree.

So this is how it happens.

Jonathan had earned a college degree, learned to fly airplanes, and fought for his country on the other side of the world.

But, never, not once, had he found *the right girl.* And here she was. She'd dropped down into his bedroom.

If that wasn't divine intervention, he didn't know what was.

Now all he had to do was get himself back alive and in one piece from Vietnam – again. And keep Vaughn here in the meantime.

Fortunately, he had until after the new year to convince her to stay.

He lifted the ax off his shoulder and rested it on the ground.

"Are you sure?" He asked. "With all these trees, at least a hundred, how did you pick this one?"

"Sometimes you just know these things," she said, a mischievous smile on her face.

He nodded. Sometimes you just had to go with your gut.

He almost didn't notice at first as the first snowflake floated down and landed on his sleeve. But another quickly followed.

She noticed then, too, and held out her hand. "It's snowing!" She said.

He grinned. A rare snowfall in Natchez. At Christmas time. While hunting for a Christmas tree.

It was one of those rare magical moments in time. A time when everything seemed to come together.

He released the ax, letting it fall to the ground, and moved toward her. His gaze must have been intense because she took two steps back, standing behind the tree limbs.

Reaching her quickly, her took her elbows in his hands, pulling her toward him. He placed one hand on her cheek and, placing a finger under her chin, tilted her face toward his. Her lips parted slightly, and her eyes fluttered closed.

He moved forward until his breath mingled with hers. His lips were so close to hers, he could almost feel them. A snowflake landed on his cheek.

He pulled her against him and touched his lips against hers. He felt, more than heard, the little gasp that escaped on a breath.

Neither one of them moved as the seconds ticked past. They were locked there in their own little snow globe.

Jonathan felt his world tilt and shift beneath him.

Vaughn was the girl he wanted.

She was one he'd been waiting for.

CHAPTER 19

Vaughn held the door open while Jonathan brought the tree inside. It hadn't looked nearly so big growing outside in the wild .

He'd chopped it down, loaded it onto the back of the truck, and now he stood staring at it. The tree stretched across the foyer.

"Will it fit?" She asked.

"It might be too tall."

"What do we need to do?" She asked.

"I'll build a frame for it, then we'll stand it up. If it's too tall, I'll cut the top out."

"Too bad we can't measure it first," Vaughn commented.

He shrugged. "We could, but I think it'll fit."

The clock chimed twelve times.

"Are you hungry?" He asked.

"A little," she nodded. The crisp cool air had stirred her appetite.

"If you'll make some sandwiches, I'll go out and cut some boards."

She wanted to watch him cut the boards. She wanted to see

how everything worked, but she also wanted a moment to think about what had happened in the woods.

She wanted a moment to cherish the magical moment when he'd kissed her with snowflakes falling all around them.

She'd never been kissed before. And she could still feel the light pressure of his lips against hers.

She nodded and left him to go into the kitchen. She'd watched him make sandwiches yesterday, so it was easy enough to replicate what he'd done. She opened the package of bread and took out four slices, putting them on a plate that she took from the cupboard.

She then opened what she thought of as the cold box and took out other things needed for the sandwich.

Since she'd never been kissed before, she had nothing to compare to that moment with Jonathan. It was all she could think about. His soft, firm lips on hers. She couldn't help but wonder if this meant they would get married.

Would he want to kiss her again? Her thoughts swirled as she opened another package and took out slices of turkey. Putting them in a pan, she slid them into the little oven sitting on the counter. She mimicked what she had seen Jonathan do and turned a little knob. She smiled when the oven began to heat.

While she waited, she pulled a little book from a stack of mail and flipped through the pages. It was obviously a catalog selling clothing and other items. All the ladies wore dresses that were too short. Like the ones Jonathan had bought her, they stopped at their knees. The images showed them wearing these dresses out in public. This America was much different than anyone had warned her about.

She placed the warm turkey on the bread, cut a tomato, and put that, too, on the sandwich.

She felt safe here with Jonathan. There was so much about

this world that she didn't know about, but it didn't seem to matter. She stood and stared at the calendar. 1969.

There was so much to learn. Like the motorized truck. The telephone. The short dress.

Taking the sandwiches, she took them into the foyer where Jonathan was nailing boards around the bottom of the tree.

When she walked into the room, he stopped and looked up to smile at her. Her heart skipped a beat, and she smiled back.

Sitting next to the fir tree, with the snow falling outside, they ate sandwiches she had made.

Vaughn wanted this moment to never end.

CHAPTER 20

Jonathan watched the snowfall coming down like rain now. He hoped his friend decided not to stop by. The weather was too bad for travel.

Besides, he wanted to keep Vaughn all to himself. He didn't want their idyllic time to be interrupted by a guest.

He turned and looked at the tree. After they ate lunch, they'd stood the tree up. The top of the tree was bent over against the ceiling by only a few inches. Not enough to worry about.

After hauling the trunk stuffed full of Christmas decorations downstairs, Jonathan left Vaughn sorting them while he brought in firewood and built a fire in the fireplace. When he came back, she had decorations sorted all over the floor.

If there was one thing he could say for her, she was organized. She'd organized the clothes in his bureau and now the Christmas decorations. He wondered if she would like to have lights for the tree, but given her austere tendencies, he decided to see what she would do without lights.

"Do you have everything you need?" He asked.

She lifted her gaze from where she sat on the floor surrounded by hand-carved little toy decorations and delicate glass balls. "I'll be needing your help," she said.

Her long dark hair was pulled around to fall over her left shoulder. Her eyes were bright, and, again, he was struck by how delicate her features were.

Going to her side and kneeling next to her, his pulse raced through his veins. He would do anything for her and wanted more than anything to spend time with her. "How can I help?"

"We need to get these decorations up there," she said, pointing toward the tree towering over them. "And this angel goes at the very top."

He glanced toward the top of the tree. He was going to need a ladder. He lowered his gaze back to hers. She was smiling impishly.

It was more than he could handle.

He put one hand gently behind her head and placed his lips against hers. Time ceased to exist, and the rest of the world faded away.

CHAPTER 21

Vaughn grasped Jonathan's shoulders as he leaned her back and kissed her. All thoughts left her mind as his lips pressed against hers.

He pulled back and pressed his forehead against hers.

"I have to leave in three weeks."

"For how long?" She asked, trying to focus.

"I have to be gone for a year."

She pulled away from him to better look into his eyes. "A year?" A year may as well be forever.

"There's a war," he said. "I have to fight."

"You're a soldier?"

"I'm actually a commander, but yes, I'm a soldier. After this year, my time will be up, and I don't have to be in the military anymore."

"You need me to go," she said, swallowing the panic that stirred in her throat at the impossibility of finding her way in this time.

"No," he said. "No. No. I want you to stay."

"You want me to stay here?" she asked.

"Please," he said. "Please wait for me."

She stood up and walked to the front door. Turned around. "You want me to stay here. In your house?"

"Yes."

"What will I do?"

"I don't know," he said. "What do you like to do?"

"I read and study and..." She thought about Beau and Abigail. "I'm a tutor."

"You could teach," he said, standing up and stepping over the decorations to reach her.

She shook her head. He had no idea what he was asking. Yes, she could teach. But there were too many hurdles to overcome. Hurdles she couldn't even begin to imagine.

This was not her world.

She wanted to be here with Jonathan. But not here by herself. Not for a year. An afternoon maybe. Maybe even overnight now and then.

But not a year. She was shaking her head. "I can't."

"But we have the rest of our lives once I get back."

"I'm not from here. I don't know how to survive that long. I'm not ready."

"I'll get you ready. We have three weeks."

She laughed and lowered her head. Three weeks to catch her up on hundreds of years. It wasn't possible. "I shouldn't even be here."

She saw the pain in his eyes as she said the words. But it was true.

She shouldn't be here.

She had been born in 1697. In her world, it was 1714. If she told him she had traveled through time, he would think she was crazy. She barely believed it herself, much less to ask someone else to believe it.

"It's OK," he said. "I'll get the ladder."

He turned and walked toward the storage room to get the

ladder. She'd hurt him. She saw it in his eyes before he turned around.

Her heart heavy, she went into the parlor and stood in front of the fireplace, holding her hands out to soak up the warmth from the flames.

She needed to get dressed. His friend Edward would be here soon. She would wear the black dress with the white dots. She could wear the soft trousers beneath it since it was snowing outside. If it was a fashion faux pas, she would be forgiven due to the cold weather. She would put the blue ball gown on tomorrow when they were alone. According to what she could discern, it was no longer anywhere near the current fashion.

Vaughn didn't know what to do. She wanted to be here with him. But he wanted her to wait here for a year. A whole year!

I have nothing else to do.

The realization came out of nowhere. In truth, this was the best thing. If he asked her to leave, she would be homeless. Homeless in a strange country in a strange time. Thanks be to God that she was blessed to have learned English.

She turned her back to the fire and lifted her chin. Whatever it was she needed to do to survive in this time, she could do it. She could learn. She was fluent in four languages. She could sketch. She could stitch. She could play the piano.

She could learn which buttons to press to heat her food and wash her clothes.

Vaughn could wait for one year until Jonathan returned in order to be with him.

He was more than key to her survival. She was falling in love with him.

When she heard him setting up the ladder, she went back to the foyer and stood next to him.

"Okay," she said, the word feeling strange on her lips. "I'll wait for you."

A grin broke out across his face. He reached out and took her hand in his, linking his fingers with his. "Why the sudden change of heart?" He asked.

"It was unexpected. And I was overcome with fear," she admitted.

"Don't be afraid," he said. "I'll give you a phone number you can call to reach me if you need anything at all." He pulled her against him. "Or if you're just afraid. You can talk to me on the telephone."

She pulled back and smiled at him. "A year isn't so very long," she said. "I can read about your history and catch up."

"I'll get you books from the library," he said. "You said you like to study. When I get back, you can teach me everything you've learned."

"I can do that." The heaviness lifted from her heart as she looked into his blue eyes. This man wanted her to wait for him while he fought a war.

She was blessed.

CHAPTER 22

Loud knocking at the door disturbed Jonathan and Vaughn from putting the last touches on the Christmas tree.

"It must be Edward," Vaughn said.

"It must be," Jonathan agreed. "I thought the snow would delay him." He'd hoped Edward would have skipped stopping by. He'd been looking forward to spending the evening next to the fireplace with Vaughn nestled at his side. Edward was really more of a coworker than a friend. He was a little perplexed at this unexpected visit. Edward had never come here before.

Jonathan went to open the front door. "Edward, come in." He ushered the man inside. "How did you get here in this weather?"

"I didn't have a choice. I have to be on base by morning, so I'm just stopping by on a break."

"Why the rush?" Jonathan asked.

Edward didn't answer. He was staring at Vaughn, who was putting the last of the decorations on the tree.

Jonathan squelched the urge to punch his friend for staring

at his girl as Vaughn turned and smiled at them.

Edward looked at him, his face full of questions.

"Edward, this is my girlfriend, Vaughn."

"You've been holding out," Edward said, moving toward Vaughn.

"It's nice to meet you, sir," she said, holding out her hand, palm down.

Edward took her hand, without a hitch at the unconventional greeting. "The pleasure is all mine," he said as he kissed the back of her hand.

"Why the rush to get back to base?" Jonathan asked again, wanting to boot his friend out now.

Edward released Vaughn's hand and turned back to Jonathan. He put a hand on his shoulder. "Let's talk," he said, leading Jonathan toward the parlor.

Jonathan was relieved that they were walking away from Vaughn. When they were out of earshot, he answered. "Things are escalating," he said.

"Escalating? How?"

"I'm not sure, but the rumor is we may be called back earlier than we thought."

"But we're leaving in only three weeks."

"It'll be sooner. Mark my words."

"How much sooner?"

"Not sure. Probably at least a week."

"Damn," Jonathan said, turning away and putting his palm against the back of the nearest chair. He rubbed his forehead with his other hand.

It was bad enough knowing he had to leave her right after the new year, but now he would be leaving around Christmas – in less than two weeks. It was too much to ask. He barely had time to get her ready. And now he had that much less time with her before he had to leave.

"Yeah, I wouldn't be happy either if I had to leave a girl like that."

"You've got your wife," Jonathan said. "And your baby."

"I hope this girl will wait for you, man," Edward said.

"What are you talking about?" Jonathan felt his face flush.

"I've never known you to have a girlfriend. Now you bag a hot babe like that." Edward shook his head. "I don't know. A year's a long time."

"She's not your business," Jonathan said.

"You never know. I might come home before you."

Before he knew what he was doing, he had his hands on Edward's neck and shoved him against the wall.

"Don't you ever disrespect her like that again," he said between his teeth.

Edward's eyes were wide as grunted beneath the pressure on his neck.

Stepping back, Jonathan shoved him to the floor. "Get out," he said.

Edward got to his feet and stood glaring at Jonathan. "I was just joshing, man."

"We may have to sit in a plane together, but I don't want to *ever* see you around here again, and I *never* want to hear you speak of her again. *Ever.*"

Edward moved toward the door. "Geez," he said.

"If I even suspect you came near her, I will kill you."

Edward scowled at him, but hurried went out the front door, slamming it behind him.

Vaughn came to the doorway and looked at Jonathan. "Where did Edward go?"

CHAPTER 23

Vaughn had heard the scuffling coming from the parlor.

"He had to leave before the roads get any worse."

It was already dark outside, and Vaughn knew that the roads were already treacherous. She also knew that Jonathan had kicked his friend out.

Vaughn hadn't liked the way Edward looked at her. His eyes had swept her from head to toe. His smile had been overly familiar, and he'd held her hand too long. She was glad he had left.

She didn't like seeing Jonathan riled up this way, even on her account. His hands were fisted at his sides, and his face had a hint of red as he stared out the window, watching the lights from Edward's truck travel away from the house.

"Thank you," she said.

He took a deep breath, blinked, and focused on her. "For what?" He asked.

"For protecting my honor."

"Come here," he said, holding out a hand toward her.

She went to him and wrapped her arms around his waist.

As he put his arms around her, she leaned her cheek against his chest. This man set her heart aflutter and made her feel safe.

The fire crackled behind them in the fireplace, and the clock chimed seven times. A blanket of snow covered the house.

Vaughn sighed.

Jonathan nudged her back and found her lips with his. This kiss was different from the last. This kiss was deeper. His lips claimed hers, and his tongue caressed her lips.

Vaughn leaned into him, unable to get close enough.

He moved his lips to the side of her mouth and sent fiery tingles all through her. His lips traveled along her cheek to her earlobe. Her eyes closed, she leaned back, and pushed toward him all at the same time. Then he kissed her eyelids.

"I'm probably going to be leaving sooner than I thought," he said. Her eyes fluttered open. Why had he stopped kissing her?

"I have so much to teach you. We'll have to start tomorrow. As soon as the roads clear, I have to teach you to drive."

"Uh huh," she said, not sure what she was agreeing to. How could he even think? His kisses had her thoughts so befuddled that she could hardly focus at all.

"Vaughn," he said, pulling her to him again. "Please wait for me."

Wait for him. Vaughn would wait for him.

There was one minor problem, however. She didn't know how she came to be here to begin with. Or how long she would be here.

How could she make a promise when she didn't know if she could keep it?

CHAPTER 24

The next morning came with sunshine. There was only a light dusting of snow on the ground. Jonathan moved his sawhorses to the back veranda out of the dampness. He felt pressure to get the repairs done as soon as possible so that the house would be in good shape while he was gone. He didn't want Vaughn worrying about rotten floors or cabinet doors falling off the hinges.

Jonathan took some measurements in the kitchen to replace a cabinet door that had fallen in disrepair. Disrepair. More like falling apart. He was going to have to make a new cabinet door from scratch.

The measurements in his head, he went outside, put a board on the sawhorses, drew some lines across the boards with a pencil, and picked up the Skil-saw.

He glanced up when Vaughn appeared in the doorway, looked at the lines on the board, then back up to her. He lowered the saw and straightened up.

She'd pulled her hair up on top of her head, leaving ringlets to frame her face. And she was wearing the blue dress she'd found in the trunk.

The skirt flowed around her in volumes of silk. She was a vision from the past. From the antebellum days when ladies wore hoop skirts and men courted them.

She smiled, and his heart lodged in his throat. This dress had been made for this girl. Unlike the clothes he had bought her, this dress brought out her beauty like nothing else.

"What do you think?" She asked, coming onto the veranda and twirling around him.

He struggled to find words to describe the vision in front of him. "You're beautiful," he said. It was the only thought he could focus on.

The other thought, he couldn't say out loud. The other thought was that she would make a beautiful bride in that dress.

She moved in the dress as though she dressed this way all the time.

Jonathan had forgotten that he held the Skil-saw. It slipped from his hand and began falling. The cord, however, was wrapped around his ankle and as he went to grab it with his other hand, the switch turned on.

The unexpected loud buzz of the saw caused him to jump back. When he did, he tripped on the tangled cords, and fell onto the porch floor.

The blade of the saw sliced against his thigh on its way to the floor. He dropped it and it turned off, leaving only an echo of sound in the air.

"Mon Dieu!" Vaughn cried, racing toward him to kneel next to him.

The pain in Jonathan's thigh was like nothing else he had ever experienced. Grasping his leg, he fell to his knees.

"Jonathan!" Vaughn said, but he barely heard her. Instead he saw men falling to the ground in Vietnam as he did a flyby, bullets shooting from the plane.

His hands slick with blood, he closed his eyes against the pain.

CHAPTER 25

Vaughn was covered in blood. She swallowed the sickness at the back of her throat. She needed to stop the bleeding.

Reaching under her skirt, she found her petticoat and ripped off a strip. The material was old and ripped easily. She pushed his hands aside and began wrapping the wound.

She couldn't tell the extent of the wound, but it appeared to be flesh only. His bone appeared to be intact. That machine he'd been using could have easily cut his leg completely off.

His eyes fluttered open. "You have to get me to the hospital," he said.

"Where?" She tied off the bandage, but it was already soaked with blood.

The hospital. She glanced up, instinctively looking for a horse. She pressed her fingers against her forehead. No horses. *Stay calm and think.*

She would have to get him to the truck. Fortunately, it was parked only a few feet away.

"Come on," she said, nudging him.

He groaned.

"Help me get you up," she said, tugging at his arm. "Come on," she insisted. "I won't let you die."

They managed to get him to his feet and down the stairs. By the time they got to the truck, he had practically all his weight on her. She stared at the door to the truck. "How does it open?"

He pointed to the handle. "Pull," he said.

She opened the door and somehow managed to push him inside. He leaned his head against the back of the seat, his eyes closed again.

She dashed around to the driver's side and climbed inside. Why had she put this dress on today of all days? Once she was inside, she stared at the dashboard. Now what?

"Keys," he said.

She looked at him blankly.

"Go inside and get the keys. Hanging by the back door." His voice sounded weak.

She climbed out of the truck and, gathering her skirts up, dashed up the stairs, inside the house, and found the keys hanging on a nail by the back door.

She ran back to the truck and climbed back in.

Should she put on a fresh bandage or start driving?

It made sense to get him to the hospital as soon as possible.

Fumbling with the keys, she found one that fit into the keyhole. She turned the key and the truck roared to life.

She reached over, shook Jonathan, and said. "Help me!"

He walked her through the basics to get them moving down the driveway. Vaughn sat forward, her hands clutching the wheel, her right foot pressing on the pedal. Her left foot rested against the brake, ready to stop at any moment.

She reached the end of the driveway and stopped.

"Which way?" She asked.

Jonathan didn't answer. She shook him again. "Where's the hospital?"

He looked up, his eyes glazed over now. "That way," he said, pointing left.

She turned the wheel to the left and then pressed on the pedal that made the truck move. Another truck, this one with no bed, flew past them and honked as they passed by.

Jonathan sat up. "Stay on the right side of the road. When you get into town, you'll see signs pointing you to the hospital."

She nodded and steered the truck out of the middle of the road.

Jonathan ran his hands over the bandage, then leaned back again. He wiped the blood from his hands onto his pants.

Vaughn pressed her foot down harder on the pedal, and the truck sped up. Her knuckles turned white against the wheel, and she focused all her concentration on driving.

As they drew close to what must be the town, the traffic picked up. There were trucks of all shapes and sizes rushing around them. She didn't know if Jonathan had passed out, but either way, it took all her focus to steer the truck.

CHAPTER 26

"Pull over," Jonathan said.

"What?" Vaughn said through clenched teeth.

She had obviously never driven before, and she had no idea where to go. He sat up a little straighter and took a deep breath. Some of the initial shock had worn off. He could still feel his toes, so his leg hadn't been severed.

"Pull over here," he said, pointing to a parking lot.

After she pulled over, he scooted over to the middle and put the truck in park. "Climb over," he said.

She looked askance at him. "If you're going to drive," she said, "I'll go around."

"Okay," he agreed. While she climbed out of the truck, he managed to pull himself into the driver's seat. He waited until she was safely back inside before he took off.

He was driving much too fast, but he wanted to make sure he made it to the hospital before he passed out.

He pulled up to the ER and turned off the motor. "Go inside and tell them you need help," he said.

Out of the corner of his eyes, he saw a blur of blue before he passed out.

CHAPTER 27

Jonathan lay in a hospital bed, hooked up to a machine. Vaughn sat in a chair next to him.

They hadn't let her in at first, but that had been a few hours ago.

They'd cleaned him up, but she still had blood all over her dress. Someone, a doctor or nurse, she didn't know, had told her that he was going to be all right. They said he'd been in shock, but the wound would heal in a few days.

She leaned across the bed and ran her fingers through his hair. Whatever they had given him had caused him to sleep for hours.

She refused to leave him until he woke up.

This man had become dear to her in such a short time.

She linked her fingers though his hand and chastised herself… again. She never should have gone outside when he was working. He'd nearly lost a leg, or worse, because she'd been so irresponsible as to distract him while he worked.

Exhausted, she crawled onto the bed and curled up next to him.

"Vaughn," she heard her name and jerked her head up. She must have fallen asleep.

"Jonathan," she said. "You're awake."

"Is this Heaven?"

"Hardly."

"You did it," he said. "You saved my life."

"On the contrary," she said. "I nearly cost you your life."

He shook his head. "No, my love, I was the idiot."

She smiled. "We were idiots together."

He smiled back, and her heart beat much too quickly.

"Am I going to walk again?" He asked.

"They said it was minor. That you went into shock."

"I thought I'd cut my damn leg off."

"You almost did. That thing – that Skil saw – is quite dangerous."

"I was hoping to have my tour delayed a bit. I guess it didn't work."

"They said it won't affect your ability to be a soldier."

He ran a hand along her cheek. "That's unfortunate."

She closed her eyes and leaned toward him. "Unfortunate. Yes."

There was a quick knock on the door, and a man in a white coat was standing at the foot of the bed. "You seem to be feeling much better," he said.

Vaughn started to move, but Jonathan wrapped his arms around her and held her next to him.

"I just woke up," Jonathan said. "How does it look?"

"You can go home," the doctor said. "But stay off that leg for three days." He looked at Jonathan over his glasses. "And don't drive home."

CHAPTER 28

Vaughn and Jonathan settled into a routine over the next couple of days. Vaughn had driven home – this time under Jonathan's watchful tutelage.

Jonathan had slept downstairs on the sofa in front of the fireplace in order to avoid going up and down the stairs.

He had shown her how to wash the blue dress in the washing machine, but that hadn't turned out so well. Not only had the stains not come out, but the material was so old that the dress had come out of the machine ripped into little more than shreds. She'd been close to tears.

"I'll never forget the way you looked wearing it," Jonathan had said, pulling her close and kissing her on the top of her head.

Jonathan's letter came on Tuesday.

Vaughn had gone to the mailbox and sat next to him as he opened his mail.

"I have to leave December 24," he said.

"But that's Christmas Eve," Vaughn said.

Jonathan nodded. He felt sick to his stomach. Not only was

he having to leave her, but he was having to leave her on Christmas Eve. It was a cruel hand life had dealt him.

"I promise I'll spend every Christmas after this making it up to you," he said, taking both her hands in his and kissing each fingertip one by one.

"I plan to hold you to that, Jonathan Becquerel," Vaughn said, her eyes fluttering closed as he pressed his lips against hers.

CHAPTER 29

Two days before it was time for Jonathan to leave, he insisted that she make a trial run to the grocery store.

"But we have enough food," she said. She didn't like driving the truck. She didn't like the other trucks – Jonathan had informed her that some of them were called cars. She hadn't thought far enough ahead to worry about what would happen when she didn't have enough food. Indeed, there was so much food in the pantry, she imagined that she could live off of it for at least the whole year.

Nonetheless, he insisted that she would need bread, milk, eggs, and other *perishables.* Since he had no chickens and no cows, she assumed he knew what he was talking about and acquiesced.

"Pretend I'm not with you," he said as he climbed into his side of the truck.

"How can I do that when you distract me?"

Even with him watching her, the drive went much better this time than it had when she'd driven him to the hospital.

Mostly because she didn't have to go into town. The store was on the outskirts.

She had worn her yellow dress and blended in nicely with the other ladies in the store. That much, at least, was a relief. Jonathan had helped her figure out what to buy and stood quietly by as she wrote out the check – just as he had shown her earlier at home.

The clerk, Mrs. Lawrence, had raised her eyebrows at Jonathan.

"She's good," he said.

"Then you need to take her over to the bank and put her on your account. I might not be here next time she comes in."

Jonathan and Vaughn put their groceries in the truck and using his directions, Vaughn drove them to the bank.

"You're a natural," he said, when she pulled into the parking lot and parked the car.

"I don't know about that," she said. "Maybe you can drive home."

He leaned over and kissed her on the lips. "I'll gladly drive us home. Come on, let's make you official."

He took her hand and led her inside the bank, walking up to the third of four tellers. "Hey Bob," he said.

"Hey Jonathan. I heard you were shipping out again."

"In a few days," Jonathan said. "This is my girl, Vaughn. I need to allow her access to my accounts."

"All of them?" He asked.

Jonathan thought about his friends who hadn't come home from the war. He thought about how he had no family and no heirs. He looked over at Vaughn, who smiled sweetly every time he looked at her, and was overwhelmed by the urge to protect her and take care of her. If not her, his money and property would go to the state.

He turned back to Bob. "Yes, all of them."

Jonathan and Vaughn sat in the lobby while Bob typed up the signature cards and other documents for Vaughn to sign.

"You don't have to do this," she said, keeping her voice low.

"I need to. You need to have access while I'm gone."

"I don't need much. Just give me a few coins and I'll be good until you get back. The pantry has more than enough food."

"If something happens to me while I'm over there," Jonathan said. "I want you to be taken care of."

"But why?" she asked.

He tucked her hair behind her ear and gazed into her green eyes. It was a question he couldn't answer. The decision was based strictly on emotion.

He'd begun falling for this girl the moment he'd seen her. "You put butterflies in my stomach," he said.

Her eyes widened. "Oh dear. Is that dangerous?"

He laughed, took her hand, and kissed her knuckles. "It is dangerous," he said, tapping his leg where the saw had nicked him.

"I don't. . ."

Bob called them up to the counter. Jonathan stood up and held out his hand to help Vaughn up from the couch.

He watched her as she signed her name to the documents that essentially gave her everything he owned.

Others would probably say he was insane.

When he got back from this interminable war, he would have to convince her to be his wife.

CHAPTER 30

Biting her lip, Vaughn signed her name with the magical pen that held a never-ending supply of ink. She no longer questioned such things. She caught only a glimpse of the words neatly printed on the documents, but it was enough to tell her that Jonathan was a wealthy man.

He was putting an inordinate amount of trust in her. Perhaps she should tell him that she wasn't from this time. Somehow it seemed like he had a right to know.

He would doubtless think her insane.

When he returned from the war, she would tell him. She didn't want him to worry while his life was in danger. Already, she'd caused him enough distraction with the Skil-saw incident.

Jonathan, it seemed, was easily distracted.

She wondered what he would want in exchange for allowing her access to his money. Did he want her to be his mistress?

She knew of many women from a similar penniless background who led that kind of life. Mother Agnes had told her that women did what they had to do to survive. She did not pass judgment.

If only she could talk to the nuns, they could help her understand this time travel predicament and help her understand what she should do.

They signed the papers and started home. Vaughn sat quietly as Jonathan drove home. It was growing dark now, and she looked in awe at the bright lights. When she asked Jonathan about them, he said they were Christmas decorations.

Only twenty minutes after they got inside, two cars pulled up in front of the house, and about ten people stood at the front door when Jonathan opened it.

Vaughn heard the singing and went to investigate. He pulled her close and whispered, "They're caroling," in her ear.

When they began singing *Hark! The Herald Angels Sing,* Vaughn felt a rush of familiarity shoot through her. It was a song she had sung every Christmas with the nuns. Her eyes stung with unshed tears as she raised her chin to smile at Jonathan.

When *God Rest Ye Merry Gentlemen* came next, Vaughn felt a tear slide down her cheek. Her heart swelled with happiness that she had found Jonathan here in this unfamiliar world. A world where some things, like familiar Christmas carols and love had not changed.

When the carolers had climbed back in their cars and driven off, Vaughn took his hand and pulled him into the parlor.

"There's something I have to tell you," she said.

CHAPTER 31

When Jonathan had joined the Air Force, he'd wanted to see the world. He'd wanted to get out of Natchez, Mississippi and see what else was out there. He'd even imagined that he'd meet the perfect woman, marry her, and have perfect kids.

That was eight years ago.

Now he didn't want to leave his family's home. He didn't want to go back out in the world.

He wanted to stay right here.

With this woman.

Forever.

He now knew that the rest of world, no matter how big it was, was no better than his corner of the world.

His corner of the world had Vaughn in it. And that was all that mattered.

It was just one year. One year and he would never have to leave again without her.

"You'll be here when I get back?" He asked for the hundredth time.

"Yes," she said.

"You promise?"

"I promise," Vaughn said, her eyes bright with unshed tears.

Despite her promise, he knew it was one she may not be able to keep.

They'd talked about it one time. One time was enough. As his grandmother always said, *Don't buy trouble.*

Simple words from a simple woman, but no truer words were ever spoken. Don't worry about things that may or may not happen.

He pulled her against him into a hug. "You'll call me if you need anything," he said.

She nodded against his chest.

"The number is on the refrigerator."

"I know."

"I love you," he murmured against her ear.

"I love you," she said so faintly, he wasn't sure he heard.

The clock inside the house chimed five times. It was much too early to be up, much less headed out into the world. But he had to go.

"Wait for me," he said, pulling back, looking into her green eyes.

"I will," she said, but the tears were falling down her cheeks now.

He took both her hands in his and squeezed. He turned, still holding her hand. She took two steps with him until she reached the top of the stairs. He squeezed her hand again and released it.

Her hand falling from his, he walked down the front stairs of the house with a lump in his throat. Nothing had ever felt so very wrong to him. When he reached the bottom of the stairs, he turned around and, walking backwards, raised his hand to her in a wave goodbye. She lifted her hand in return. He would hold on to this memory of her standing there. *Someone to come home to.*

A flurry of movement to his right caught his attention. He turned to see a covey of quail bolting into the sky. He didn't know what had startled them. They made an impressive image with the fog swirling all around them as they rushed toward the sky. Just as he would be doing in his airplane.

He turned his gaze back to the porch.

Vaughn was gone.

EPILOGUE

December 1839

"It's going to storm," Camille Becquerel said, her gaze on the dark clouds above.

Vaughn Dupree followed the girl's gaze. Yes. It was going to storm. But it wasn't just the clouds. There was an electricity in the air.

A danger.

Just like it had been so very long ago – another lifetime, but Vaughn's nerve cells tingled with the memory of life and death.

The storms like this one came every few years. There had been two last year. All from the southeast. Vaughn suspected that they were the result of hurricanes. But with no weather channel, she was limited in news from the outside world.

"Do you want to go inside?" Camille asked.

"Not yet," Vaughn said, enjoying the cool wind on her face. There was nothing she liked better than a storm.

A storm brought promises. And memories. And options.

When the rain started, the first fat drop falling on her hand, Vaughn went indoors, Camille on her heels.

Vaughn went into the bedroom of her little cottage and opened the armoire. On the second to the bottom shelf, beneath her nightgowns, was a hatbox. The hatbox blended in with her collection of gowns, crinolines, shawls, and other personal clothing items.

Camille sat on the bed and watched as Vaughn pulled the hatbox out and set it on the bed.

It had been many years since she'd opened the box. Her hands trembled a little as she removed the lid and set it aside.

First, she picked up the stockings. A little outdated according to her granddaughter, Erika, but nonetheless, a staple in Vaughn's mind.

Next she picked up the little black sheath dress with its sweetheart neckline. So simple, yet so elegant. And so very modern. The smooth, thick cotton felt foreign to her hands as she held it against her. Would she still be able to wear it? Things had… shifted a bit with age.

"Is that your chemise?" Camille asked.

Vaughn's lips curved in a smile. "This is my dress."

Camille's eyes widened. "Not much surprises me anymore," she said, running a hand along the short hem of the dress. She lifted her eyes to Vaughn's. "But you wear this in public? With nothing over it?"

"It's quite fashionable," Vaughn told her.

Camille had become a most interesting friend. Vaughn's granddaughter, Erika, was busy with her newborn infant while her husband oversaw the cotton crop. Vaughn's grandson, Bradley, Camille's husband spent much of his days on his steamboat ferrying people and supplies from dock to dock. She smiled at the unlikely occupation of her grandson who had been an airplane pilot in another time.

So Camille had her days to herself. And, it seems, a fascination with Vaughn. Vaughn had lived many years of her life here in the nineteenth century, but she had also lived many years in the future.

Vaughn smiled to herself as she considered this. Perhaps someday she'd tell Camille about how she'd started out in France in the 1700s. An orphan seeking her place in the world.

Thunder crashed in the distance. There may not be time, though, Vaughn thought. She needed to make sure her diaries were placed in good hands.

"I need to show you something," Vaughn said, beckoning Camille to her armoire.

With Camille standing beside her, she stood on her tiptoes and lifted a blanket from the top shelf.

Camille gasped. "What are those?" she asked.

Camille read everything she could get her hands on. Yes, Camille was the right choice for safekeeping her diaries.

"My diaries," Vaughn said. "A chronicle of my life and my reflections over time." Turning, she gazed into Camille's lovely eyes.

1838 was Vaughn's favorite time period so far. There would be a war soon. The war between the states. But Vaughn would be long gone before that happened. She felt fortunate she wouldn't have to live through that destruction.

She'd been born in 1697 and had fond memories of the first seven years of her life. Once she'd gone to the orphanage, the world had become a cold dark place. But at seventeen, she'd escaped to America. That's where her life had changed forever.

She'd spent most of her life in the last part of the twentieth century and early twenty-first century. Those had been interesting times and she had put down roots.

Those roots had followed her here, she mused, in the form of her grandchildren, Erika and Bradley.

And with them things changed. Vaughn had never really been accepted into the Becquerel family. She frightened people.

Not Nathaniel, of course, but others. Fortunately, Nathaniel had made provisions for her care before he died.

Vaughn couldn't explain why she'd come back here in her later days. Perhaps to feel closer to Nathaniel. Or perhaps to be closer to her heritage.

Whatever it was, didn't matter now. What was done was done.

But then Bradley had brought pictures. And Vaughn's loneliness had become less bearable.

Once Erika had come through the rift, Vaughn believed that her time had passed. There was no science to her theory. She only went with her gut.

But then Bradley had come through. Bradley's time-travel was clearly precipitated by love. The time travelling had always happened here in the plantation house. But with Bradley, it had happened the first time in New Orleans. That's where he'd found Camille.

Camille was a sweet, loving girl who was open minded about just about everything. Vaughn truly believed that Camille would have been quite at home in the twenty-first century.

And then Bradley had gone and brought photographs. Vaughn's heart had tripped at the sight of her husband, Jonathan. Even in the photographs she could see the sadness in his eyes.

He missed her.

And she missed him.

Vaughn could only speculate about her purpose here. Perhaps it had been to be here for Erika and Bradley. To help them adjust to the time period. Erika had struggled more than Bradley, but then these times were easier for boys. And Erika's husband Charles had been betrothed to another. Bradley had done quite well on his own.

Vaughn was old. She wouldn't be around forever. She had to do what was best for her.

Lightening flashed a few feet from where she sat next to Camille.

"It's going to be a bad one," Camille predicted.

"I agree," Vaughn said. "In fact, let's go up to the big house, shall we?"

Camille's eyes widened. Vaughn never went to the big house – the main plantation house. She stayed there in her own little cottage. "Okay," Camille said, using the language Erika had taught her. "We'll have to hurry though or we'll get soaked." Already, the rain was falling steadily.

"Let's go," Vaughn said, and together they began the walk to the big house.

Vaughn pulled the hood up on her cloak and walked slowly. She was forgiven due to her age. But in truth, she wondered if this was last time she would walk in this time. She would miss the quietness.

They went up the stairs to the front door. As a member of the household, Camille was allowed to go inside without knocking. Vaughn followed.

Villars appeared in the foyer. His eyes widened when he saw her. "Mistress Vaughn," he said. "Welcome."

"Thank you, Villars," Vaughn said. The servants were afraid of her. They believed she practiced the voodoo magic.

"Would you like to go into the parlor?" he asked. "Shall I summon Miss Erika?"

"No. No. Don't bother Erika. She's busy with the baby. Camille and I just wanted to come in out of the rain. The parlor will be just fine."

"Would you like some tea or cool water?" he asked.

"Tea would be lovely," she said.

Villars went down the hallway and Camille started toward the parlor.

Vaughn, however, stopped in front of the grandfather clock and tipped the hood back on her cloak. The steady ticking of the clock soothed her soul. It echoed in her head even when she was in her own cottage, though she knew she probably imagined it. She couldn't possibly hear it so far away. The clock had marked the hours during the birth of her child and punctuated her lovemaking with Jonathan… and with Nathaniel.

The clock represented time itself. And time had played a more significant part in Vaughn's life than anyone could ever imagine.

Turning, she followed Camille into the parlor. Villars brought cold tea and poured it into two glasses.

Vaughn took her glass to the window and watched as the rain came down in torrents now. They had barely made it here before the sky opened and the downpour started.

The clouds were dark. Some would call them angry, but Vaughn was drawn to the storms. In some ways, she'd been born from storms.

At the sound of a baby's coo, Vaughn turned to her granddaughter and great-granddaughter. The very idea of having a great-grandchild was almost more than she could wrap her head around.

"Grandmother Vaughn," Erika said, breathless from rushing down the stairs. "I saw you from the window."

Vaughn went to her and took the baby, Arabella, in her arms. Arabella cooed and smiled back at Vaughn. Vaughn didn't care if the smile was a reflex or not. She loved that this baby looked happy. This baby would have a happy childhood. She would be an adult before war tore apart the country. She would grow up in a life of luxury.

When Arabella got to her twenties, the south would be ripped to shreds by the Civil War and life would be difficult. But if Vaughn had learned nothing else, it was that worry was a useless mental activity.

Worry and dread had no place in everyday life.

"Are you okay?" Erika asked. "You never come to the house."

Vaughn handed the baby back to her mother. "I wanted to see my great-grandchild," she said. It wasn't a complete lie. She always wanted to see little Arabella. Leaving the baby was going to be the hardest part.

"Well," Erika said, "Little Arabella is teething, I think. Only just a few minutes ago, she quieted."

"She's four months. It's time," Vaughn said.

"Can I hold her?" Camille asked.

"Of course," Erika said, handing the baby over to Camille. "In fact," Erika said, "I was just about to take a bath. My water should be ready by now. Would you two mind watching her for a little bit?"

"I'll watch her anytime," Camille said, gazing lovingly down at Arabella.

As Erika left, Vaughn was drawn back to the window. The lightening was closer now, but Vaughn didn't mind.

She wasn't afraid of lightening. She heard Camille cooing to the baby behind her.

The grandfather clock tolled the hour. Two o'clock. Only two chimes. She sighed and leaned her forehead against the cool glass.

The loneliness sweep through her more fiercely than before.

A movement in the rain caught her attention. She lifted her head and watched a horse and rider approach. Even through the rain, she could tell who it was.

It was her grandson, Bradley. He wore his captain's uniform. A little different from a modern-day pilot's uniform, but it flattered him nonetheless.

She turned, happy to be the bearer of good news. "Camille," she said. "Bradley is back early. Probably due to the storms."

Camille jumped and stood, indecision wrapped around her as she held Arabella close.

"Here," Vaughn said. "I'll hold Arabella. You go out on the porch and greet your husband."

Camille handed off the baby and dashed out front into her husband's arms. Vaughn smiled. She was sure to have a second great-grandchild before long. She was surprised Camille wasn't expecting already, the way those two loved on each other.

The baby began to fret, doubtless from being jostled too much. Vaughn put Arabella on her shoulder and paced around the parlor. Thunder crashed above them.

Vaughn moved away from the windows. She didn't mind the lightening, but the baby was different. She wouldn't put the baby in harm's way. She walked toward the foyer – fewer windows.

Camille and Bradley's laughter floated from the porch.

Vaughn stopped to shift the baby and she quieted. Vaughn stood still, not wanting to disturb her.

Lifting her gaze, she stood face to face with the grandfather clock.

She'd always found the steady ticking to be soothing. But…

The room lit up with lightening.

Vaughn lowered her head and squeezed the baby to her as the thunder rattled the house.

Then it was quiet.

The storm would not have passed so quickly.

She no longer heard the rain splashing against the door. No thunder.

A low hum replaced the sounds of the storm.

She lifted her gaze and steadied herself.

Arabella cooed softly, her little hands grabbing at the ties on Vaughn's dress.

Vaughn's eyes strayed to the stairway.

And she caught her breath.

She squeezed her eyes tightly closed, but when she opened them, he was still there.

Two steps from the bottom, his hand on the rail, Jonathan stood watching her. He had aged since she'd last seen him. But the sight of him sent a girlish thrill through her heart.

Neither of them moved.

He mouthed her name. Closed his eyes a moment, before opening them again.

"I've died then," she heard him say to himself.

She couldn't help it. She smiled.

"Jonathan. You haven't died. It's me."

Jonathan's eyes widened.

"I don't…" He stopped, his gaze stalling on the baby Vaughn had all but forgotten she held.

"Jonathan," she said, stepping toward him. Then she was in his arms. The baby wiggled and cooed between them. She didn't know if the tears were hers or his.

But it didn't matter.

She was home.

Sliding his hands to her elbows, Jonathan leaned back to look at Arabella. "Who?" he asked.

Vaughn followed his gaze to their great-grandchild wiggling in her arms.

She lifted her gaze to his. "Uh oh."

Want more time travel?
How about a bonus short story?

GET MY BONUS SHORT STORY
https://BookHip.com/RWBMXGP

Turn the page for a Preview of
A Wish Upon a Star...

A WISH UPON A STAR PREVIEW

Prologue
1814

A flash of lightning lit up the sky and a crash of thunder followed. It sounded like the world was exploding.

It wasn't raining yet, but it wouldn't be long. Rain would follow.

The animals had gone to ground. He heard nothing other than the storm. No frogs. No crickets.

The air was filled with electricity, magnifying the scent of the magnolia blossoms along the path.

Zachary Champlain sat on a wrought iron bench just outside his cousin's house. The Becquerel house. Built in the latter part of the eighteenth century by his great Uncle Nathaniel.

Already, the house was rife with history.

Uncle Nathaniel lived in a cottage—a smaller replica of the main house—not far from here with his wife, Vaughn.

Even though Uncle Nathaniel had built the main house, he'd never lived there, choosing to stay to himself.

Most considered him to be a madman.

Though no one really knew for sure, the story was that he lived there in his cottage with his wife Vaughn.

Vaughn also had a reputation for being… unusual. Sometimes years would pass and no one would see Vaughn at all.

Zachary didn't see anything odd or unusual in either of them. The thing that struck him most was how in love they seemed.

Zachary, as his parents' only male child *needed* to marry. But as a man of marriable age, he *wanted* to marry a woman he loved.

Father insisted that love wasn't necessary in a marriage. His mother suggested that love came softly.

Zachary took that to mean that though his parents weren't in love when they married, they grew to love each other over time.

Zachary didn't want to take that chance.

He wanted a modern woman. Not only a woman he was attracted to, but a woman he could have conversations with. A woman whose company he enjoyed.

On top of all that, Zachary needed an heir.

His parents had all but given up on finding Zachary a wife near their home in Birmingham.

Hence, this trip to Natchez.

Father hoped that Zachary would find someone here who suited him.

Zachary was the least concerned and saw this active search his parents were on as unnecessary and not a bit annoying.

He believed that when he saw the right girl, he would know.

With the lightning getting closer, Zachary looked up toward the moon.

And that's when he saw it.

A star shooting across the sky.

He closed his eyes and wished upon a shooting star.

Chapter 1

Anna Becquerel sat on the neon pink cushion in the window seat of her darkened second-floor bedroom. Her chin rested on her knees. Her eyes were closed, but she knew that the lightning flashes were getting closer. She felt more than heard the ensuing rumble of thunder.

Chicago blared through the headphones of her Sony Walkman, reflecting all the pain and heartbreak that welled inside her.

Her freshman algebra book lay open on her desk, her homework forgotten for the time being. A half-eaten bag of Lays potato chips crunched beneath the silent footsteps of her cat, Remie.

Snuggling deep in the varsity letter jacket that was three times too big for her, she could still smell his deep woodsy cologne with scents of cedar and cinnamon.

Samuel. The guy she'd loved since senior year of high school. They'd dated occasionally, but apparently they weren't as close as Anna had imagined.

He was five years older, a student at Auburn University, training as an airplane pilot. It had been love at first sight for Anna. She'd fallen hook, line, and sinker.

But now, the crumpled newspaper article clutched in her right hand told her that the endless depth of their love had all been one-sided. The Cinderella story of their romance had all been her imagination.

Samuel Hutchins had just married a girl named Samantha. Samuel and Samantha.

How cute.

It was just like she'd learned in her intro to psychology

class. People whose names started with the same first letter were more likely to date and stay together.

Samuel and Anna never had a chance when there was a Samuel and Samantha in the picture.

He hadn't even bothered to tell her that he was seeing someone else, much less engaged.

Married.

Her heart broke a little more as she imagined them on their cruise to the Bahamas. The article didn't leave much to the imagination.

She remembered clearly the night he'd told her about the ice bar on the cruise ship. *You'll love their martinis. I'll take you there someday.*

Instead he was taking someone else. Sharing that experience with someone other than Anna.

Anna's life was over. She would never date anyone again. She would dedicate her life to her career. Maybe she would change her major from math to something more humanitarian.

Or maybe science. Maybe she would spend her days tucked away in a lab doing research.

Whatever she decided to do, didn't really matter. Things couldn't get any worse.

Chapter 2

Anna woke the next morning with a little smile on her face. She was home from college for the weekend. Everything was good. The air coming in through the window she'd left open a couple of inches smelled clean and fresh after last night's storm.

That little moment of happiness lasted for all of about two seconds.

Then everything came crashing back.

Samuel Hutchins was married.

Her life was over.

With the much too happy sunlight streaming in through her window, she pulled the blanket over her head and lay perfectly still, not wanting to face the day.

The house was too quiet. Her Momma always made omelets and bacon when Anna was home for the weekends.

Momma started her days early. She would come in just as the sun began to lighten the sky and wake her.

Anna lowered the blanket and blinked against the sunlight.

Everything was wrong.

The house was quiet. Her dad was always outside with the lawnmower or his hammer. Or if was raining, he'd be inside working. And whether he used a drill or a staple gun, his work was never quiet.

There was no scent of bacon and coffee drifting up from the kitchen.

A shot of panic shot through her.

Someone had come in and killed her parents. Or there had been a gas leak and they lay dead in their room. Or…

Anna pulled herself back from the ledge and threw back the blanket. There had to be a logical explanation. She changed into jeans and a sweatshirt and slipped into her worn, comfortable sneakers.

She didn't bother to brush her teeth or her hair. Maybe they were sick. *Stop it.*

Rushing into the upstairs hallway, the first thing she heard was the ticking of the grandfather clock. It had been in the family forever and her dad wound it every morning. He was nothing if not consistent.

Okay. She took a deep breath. He'd wound the clock, so they weren't dead.

Still. Something wasn't right.

She padded down the stairway and went straight to the kitchen in the back. No sign of anyone there.

She then headed back to her father's study. The door was closed.

He never kept his door closed.

She made a cursory knock as she pushed the door open.

Daddy, her strong brave father, sat on the sofa, his head bent, his hands over his face.

"Daddy?" She whispered. Her pulse was through the roof. She didn't allow any of her thoughts to settle.

She looked up and she saw raw pain in his eyes. He looked surprised to see her. As though he'd forgotten she was even home. "Anna."

She tried to move forward into the room, but her feet were glued to the floor and her hands gripped the edge of the door, keeping her upright.

"Come." He patted the empty space on the sofa next to him. "Sit."

In a daze, she did as he said. "Where's Momma?" she asked softly. So softly he probably didn't even hear her.

He scrubbed his hands over his face. "She's not here."

What was he saying? "I don't understand. Is she hurt?"

"No." He stared toward the window. The clock chimed nine times. Nine o'clock already. By now, Anna should have already had her homework well underway if not completed. Her mother would be on the back veranda puttering with her plants or baking something in the oven.

"Daddy. Where's Momma?" When he didn't answer, she stood up. She'd go look for her mother herself.

"You won't find her." He turned back to face Anna now.

Anna shook her head. "You said she's not hurt." Her knees trembled with weakness. And her voice wobbled. "Is she…?"

Her father's shoulders dropped. He shook his head, but only slightly. He patted the couch next to him again.

She dropped onto the couch. She kept her gaze on his and was close enough now to see the unshed tears in his eyes.

"She went back. In time."

In time. The words swirled through her mind. Back in time.

She couldn't think. The words made no sense. Daddy wasn't making sense.

And she still didn't know where her mother was.

Daddy picked up a piece of metal from the end table. He held it out for her.

She blinked and took it from his hand. It was an old photograph. Her mother called it a daguerreotype.

Her mother sometimes tried to talk to her about history and such. Anna had no interest in the past. She was much more concerned with her Walkman and going to the movies and talking on the phone with her friends.

Since she'd gone away to college at Louisiana Tech, she was more focused on the future than ever. She hadn't settled on a major yet, but it would be something in the sciences. Maybe medical technology or marine biology or maybe even genetics. There were so many options that she'd gone with her advisor's recommendation and not settled on anything definite yet.

One of the generic degree requirements was psychology. She found it interesting enough, but it only confirmed her decision to stay away from the soft sciences. Anna liked things that were black and white.

Her father's words definitely were not invoking the definition of a tangible science.

"What is this?" she asked.

"Look at it."

Anna lowered her gaze and focused on the photograph. It was a black and white picture of two women, both wearing full long dresses. "Who are they?" she asked.

Daddy pointed to the woman on the left. "That's your mother."

Anna squinted. She could see a resemblance to her

mother. Except that Momma wore her hair down. The woman in the picture had her hair pulled back. "Maybe. How do you know?"

"See that cameo at her neck?"

Anna saw a familiar looking white cameo pinned at the neck of the woman's gown. "It looks a little like Momma's."

"It's the one I gave her."

Anna looked sideways at her father, then back to the photograph. "Is this the one you had made that looks like her?"

Daddy nodded. "It looks like it to me."

Anna shrugged. "Okay. Maybe she went to one of those places that takes old photos. You know where people dress up in old clothes and stuff."

Daddy shook his head. She looked back up at him. "Who's the other woman?"

"I don't know."

The young woman standing next to the one Daddy claimed was Momma looked a lot like Momma.

Everyone said Anna favored her father. Unlike her mother, she had lovely natural blonde hair and fuller, softer facial features. She definitely got her crooked grin from him.

"Do I have a secret sister somewhere?"

"Ha." Daddy took the photograph from her and set it back on the end table. "Anna. This is going to be difficult for you to hear."

Anna's breath caught in her throat.

"Your mother was born in another century."

"That's not possible." Anna said flatly and sat back. Daddy had always been so stable.

"Unfortunately it is."

Anna made an effort to set some of her trepidation aside. She needed to listen to her father. She needed to find out where her mother really was. It was also quite possible that her father had finally lost it. Daddy had fought in Vietnam and

Anna had heard the stories of Vietnam veterans who lost touch with reality.

Maybe she needed to learn more about psychology after all. If Daddy was going to need mental health treatment, she needed to speak the language.

She took a deep, cleansing breath. "When did this happen?"

"Last night."

"During the thunderstorm?"

He nodded.

"How do you know?"

He hesitated. She could almost see his thoughts swirling, trying to decide what to tell her. "I saw her."

Anna shuddered. Her mother was prone to flights of fancy. When Anna was little, Momma would take her up in the attic to explore old trunks. That was before Anna figured out she liked new and modern and found excuses, like most teenagers, not to hang out with her mother in the attic listening to ghost stories.

Her father had always seemed level-headed. Sometimes he would watch her mother as though if he looked away, she would disappear.

Dread wound its way up her back and reached for her heart.

Anna clutched her hands together in her lap to keep them from trembling. "What do you mean?" she whispered.

"I saw her standing at the foot of the staircase, staring at the grandfather clock. I called out to her, but she didn't answer. I started walking toward her." His chin trembled a little. "Then she was gone."

Anna refused to accept his words at face value. "Did you look for her?"

Daddy reached out and put a hand over hers. His palms were calloused from working with wood around the house. There was always something to repair or replace. A railing.

Worn floor planks. He was retired from the army. So between being retired and having spent four years in Vietnam, he was well taken care of by the government.

"I watched her," he said. "I watched her disappear in front of me."

I must remain calm. Even as she forced herself to focus, her stomach clenched. She might be sick, but it had to wait. "Is this the first time?" she asked, her voice strained.

Daddy took his hand off hers, and pressed his palms against his eyes. "Do you remember what happened when you were in kindergarten?"

"When Momma went to visit her sick friend… in Greenland… and I couldn't talk to her for three months, not even at Christmas."

"Yes," Daddy said. "And then when you were in eighth grade, she had to be in the hospital for several months."

"It was six months." Anna sat very still, but on the inside, she was trembling all over. "She wasn't allowed to use the phone and we couldn't visit her."

"She wasn't in the hospital."

"She was back in time?"

Daddy was silent. He must be struggling with his own emotions. But that part would have to wait.

"You lied to me." Her voice was flat, no accusations. Just matter of fact.

"Yes," he admitted. "I did. Your mother and I talked about it. You were young. It seemed like the best thing to do."

Anna nodded. "Like Santa Clause and the Easter Bunny."

She mentally retraced her childhood. Her youth. There was the time in kindergarten and there was the time in eighth grade. "What about two years ago? When she went to France?"

Daddy smiled wryly. "She called you twice, remember?"

Anna had been a junior in high school. She didn't

remember much more than her crush on Ronnie Wyatt. "She really went to France?"

He nodded. "She was born in France. She went to... reconnect."

Anna knew that her mother had been born in France. She spoke French fluently and could switch back and forth between English and French without a hitch. "But you said she'd been born in another century."

"That's right. She only stayed four days. Nothing was the same."

Anna leaned back, her head on the sofa, and closed her eyes.

Her father truly seemed to believe that her mother had gone back in time. She had no choice but to go along with him. For now. "When is she coming back?"

"I don't know."

"It was three months, then six months."

Daddy didn't say anything. Maybe he didn't know what to say. "So... did she decide to go on purpose or did it just happen to her?"

The area between Daddy's eyes was creased now. He didn't know how to answer her.

"I'm not sure," he said finally.

"Why would she want to go back? To leave us?"

"I don't have the answers you're looking for."

"But she is coming back, right?"

Keep Reading A Wish Upon a Star

Kathryn Kaleigh is the author of sixty-eight novels, over one hundred short stories, and many collections.

kathrynkaleigh.com

www.ingramcontent.com/pod-product-compliance
Lightning Source LLC
Chambersburg PA
CBHW030337310726
48979CB00001B/66

* 9 7 8 1 6 4 7 9 1 4 2 7 1 *